I0673696

Hard Evidence:

The Collected Bawdy Writings

Kevin Keck

M2 Press / North Carolina

Any dialogue or events ascribed to the characters in this book—those who are real and as well as those who are imagined—are entirely fictitious. I mean, who would really believe any of this stuff happened, right? This is a work purely of the author's own imagination. (With the exception of that bit about Pert Shampoo. That actually happened, and I still get mail about it from other unsuspecting onanists. Take a lesson kids: don't put Pert on your private parts.)

Oedipus Wrecked was originally published by Cleis Press in 2005.

Are You There God? It's Me. Kevin. was originally published by Bloomsbury USA in 2008.

"The Death of the Handjob"; "Sleeping with Students"; and "Interlude with the Vampire" (Nerve Mix) all originally appeared on Nerve.com in slightly different versions.

For my godfather,
John Everson (1941 - 1991)

iv

Table of Confessions

"I am not furnish'd like a beggar; therefore to beg will not become me. My way is to conjure you, and I'll begin with the women."

– Rosalind, *As You Like It*

"Lifting her skirt, she revealed her treasure. The mother lode. Pretty, I thought, but is it art?"

– Edward Abbey, *A Voice Crying in the Wilderness*

Preface

I believe the earliest of these stories—"Hard Evidence"—
was written in 1998, at the behest of Troy Fuss, who was
editor of an influential indy magazine called *Popsmear*. I'd
been turned onto *Popsmear* because it was stocked at the
coffee shop on Marshall Street where I spent most of my
time when I was a student at Syracuse. "Hard Evidence" was
not the first thing I'd sent *Popsmear*—I can't quite recall the
subject matter of that first piece, truthfully—but I was in the
habit of writing long, rambling, confessional letters to editors
in those days. I apparently unburdened my soul to Troy
concerning some rather outrageous phone bills I'd racked up
while assuaging my loneliness and innermost desires via
phone sex, and he seized upon my personal misdeeds as a
superior story to whatever nonsense I'd initially pitched him.

Shortly after that I wrote the first half of "Ass
Backwards," and while it wasn't published until three years
later when Albert Lee of *Nerve.com* read it and suggested I
lengthen it, in the meantime it made the rounds (via the
good old-fashioned United States Postal Service) to the
Features Editor for *Details Magazine*, David Keeps, and then
to *Details* West Coast editor, and I was given a much needed
ego boost with some freelance work of a less-risque nature.

However, after *Nerve.com* published "Ass Backwards," I
found myself flooded with emails from people eager to read
more of my work. (Surprisingly, many readers at that time
considered that what I wrote was "erotica" and I was the
beneficiary of some curious photographs and articles of
clothing. I suppose if you, kind reader, find these writings...
stimulating... then I am glad to oblige you. But in case you

were wondering, I have never tried to write an arousing story at any point in my career.)

And then *Nerve* paid me a staggering $300. I find money to be a solid motivator for the muses, and so I began to write a series of essays in a similar vein to "Ass Backwards," thinking of them as comic monologues and essays blended in the traditions of James Boswell, Montaigne, Charles Bukowski, Philip Roth, Woody Allen, Lenny Bruce, Richard Pryor, Henry Rollins, Gore Vidal, Joan Didion, and Bill Hicks. Believe it or not, I had maintained a curious obliviousness to the prevalent popularity of the memoir and the personal essay. I'd attended Syracuse University to study poetry; Mary Karr and Tobias Wolff were both on faculty when I arrived. What two more important memoirists could I have been in close proximity to in the 1990s? I should say none at all, and yet I consider the two of them to be *literary writers*. After all, they held academic positions, and their memoirs elicited a more elevated respect from critics. I knew memoirs had a readership—I just didn't know how vast it was.

My ignorance is, in some ways, because I have always preferred to read the classics. I don't totally ignore contemporary writers, but I've always felt that a writer ought to have a deep sense of the tradition in which he or she is working. I also hold the belief that a writer should not simply confine himself to one genre, but should hone his total craft by working in every genre. A writer should write plays, as well as poems, and novels, and essays, and journalism when the occasion calls (we must be careful to afford true journalists a separate category from that of writers in general, because the journalist makes a sacred compact with the reader that the novelist or poet does not).

I mention the initial date of composition because I am

often placed in the vast repository of other writers who also took up the form of the personal essay around the same time as I, such as David Sedaris, Sara Vowell, David Rakoff, Steve Almond, and Mike Birbiglia. I can't begin to guess why they were compelled to choose the first person narrative essay, but there is no denying a certain zeitgeist of confessional writing occurred at the turn of the 21st century. It was building through the 1990s, with memoirs and nonfiction books edging themselves onto the bestseller lists in the United States in ever increasing numbers, but in the early 2000s "truth" became *the commodity* for storytelling in American Culture. It was during this same time that television experienced a coup d'état of reality programming, and cable news outlets first questioned the integrity and honesty of their competitors by offering to serve viewers any version of *the one true reality* they might desire.

In drawing attention to this period in cultural history, when the vast audience of the world seems to be craving narrative that asserts to be the final authority on The Facts As They Actually Happened, I maintain that I never considered myself a memoirist in any literal sense. I have always thought of myself as a storyteller, and while the stories I tell may take the form of an essay, and while the events described are true in that they actually happened, I have never claimed a journalist's compact with the reader. True events are rearranged to conform to a more pleasing experience, while other details are borrowed from the lives of friends and presented as my own—not to deceive you; I would never deceive you, loyal reader, or make a fool of you. But I use deception as an actor might, to wear a mask that allows us both to gaze at something universally true, which, if looked at in the mirror, might unsettle us to rancorous depths.

When these stories were first printed, they were viewed as somewhat scandalous. Now, in the current climate of such well-wrought entertainment as *It's Always Sunny in Philadelphia, Louie, The League* and *Workaholics*, not to mention a seemingly endless stream of bawdy and badly written imitators, the pose (and prose) of personal confession in print seems relegated to the quaintness of the vinyl record.

That being said, it strikes me that throughout time, the earliest forms of subversion have arrived in print, whether delivered digitally or on paper. Thus, if these stories wind their way into your hands, by whatever means, and they give you some moment of release, either through laughter or— God help you—self abuse, and if you are comforted in knowing you are not alone—that it was, in fact, the Pert Shampoo that did that horrible thing to your genitals—then my efforts are justly rewarded.

Kevin Keck
January 10, 2014
Denver, North Carolina

from *Oedipus Wrecked**

*These stories—or essays; call them whatever pleases your categorical fancy—are not exactly in the forms as they appeared in *Oedipus Wrecked*. The selections before you are, in fact, better. In some sections I have streamlined the prose, while in other instances restoring passages that were originally excised.

Ass Backwards

When I was sixteen my mom confessed to me that she had a vibrator, which a friend had given to her, but which she never used. She just liked to keep it around "for laughs."

Within a day I found the vibrator and immediately plunged it into my own ass while in a fit of vigorous masturbation. I could spend the rest of my life in analysis and never get to the bottom of that one. In fact, I don't even know why I felt the need to stimulate my prostate-- I wasn't even aware I had one-- unless on some level my ass knew that such an act of appropriating your mother's sex toy is the modern equivalent of killing your father.

My best guess, though, is that I had read something in *Hustler* ("How was I to know that when I went to the doctor's for a routine exam, his nurse would give me a physical I would never forget!"), or I just wanted to see what was up with all those "fags."

Eventually, though, the vibrator vanished. I don't know if my mom pressed her ear to the bathroom door one night only to hear a familiar whir, or if my constant treatments of bleach (I was sanitary, if nothing else) to the vibe's surface irritated her in some fashion that she couldn't fathom and she tossed it. Either way, such a loss lead me to desperate measures, involving cucumbers, a broom handle, a fire poker (just the handle) and, in an incident I refer to simply as "The Chiquita Affair," a banana that broke off inside me. I nearly killed myself straining to get that out as quickly as possible, and let me tell you: there's nothing more fucked up than shitting a banana.

However, this was just *my* ass. I couldn't get over the fact that I was potentially a freak, and possibly violating some serious biblical code. I mean, Jews can't eat pork — surely anal delights are way higher up on the list of taboos. When I walked by people in my small town, I tried to imagine them pillaging their rectums with a variety of implements (usually garden tools), and I just couldn't do it. And somehow, when they looked back at me, I felt they knew an ice cream scooper had once protruded from my posterior. (Oh, and sickness of sicknesses, that same ice cream scooper is still nestled in one of the drawers in my parents' kitchen! I know it's been many years and numerous rinse cycles, but on those hot August afternoons when my dad suggests a chocolate sundae, I politely decline.)

This pleasure center I discovered in myself only fueled my obsession in wondering about the way other people's asses operated. I mean, for years I never came across a woman who admitted to liking (let alone having) anal sex. I read interviews with porn stars who said they reserved anal sex for their off-camera sex life, leading me to believe that fucking a girl in the ass was the Rosetta Stone of sex, performed only by women who had conditioned their sphincters in a Kegeling exercise that allowed them to siphon the jizz out of man in such a tantric fashion that would regress the lucky fellow to a womb-like state.

Because the frequency with which I got laid between sixteen and twenty-five could be measured by the appearance of comets, and because those women I did manage to bed with any regularity just seemed so loaded with vitamin D and other wholesome goodness, I never found myself in a situation where I felt comfortable saying to a girl, "So, would you mind if I fucked you in the ass tonight?"

And that lasted until I met Debra.

We were lying in bed in post-coital bliss, when I mustered the courage to ask her if she wanted to try anal sex.

"Sure."

The speed with which I was able to achieve another erection was dizzying. I grabbed a bottle of lotion from beside her bed and started lubing her up. I was generous with the lotion; I wanted things to go as smoothly as possible.

She moaned softly as I slid my finger in her ass, then two, and I thought that things had been loosened up enough. She slid a pillow under her belly and spread her legs as I got in between them, rubbing the head of my cock up and down the crack of her ass and then sliding it in. I felt more pure joy than when I graduated high school.

Then the head of my dick hit something. In my experiments with driving a dildo up my own orifice, this didn't seem right. I mean, maybe my ass was special, but I could sink my mother's vibrator pretty far in there. I pulled out a little, then pushed in again. Debra was moaning like a real champion. Things couldn't have been going better.

Except that my dick hit something again. The gravity of the situation dawned on me: the tip of my dick was in direct contact with — *something*. (I have since come to know this unfortunate circumstance as "running over a turtle.")

I immediately withdrew and leapt off the bed.

"I have to go to the bathroom," I said, and blazed a trail to the shower, haunted by thoughts of hepatitis, bacterial infections, gangrene. I didn't even wait for the water to warm up: I jumped in the shower and held my dick (which had shrunk considerably) under one of the streams of water, and then held the peehole open so it could be thoroughly rinsed.

I jumped back out of the shower, found some Q-Tips, got

back in and lathered one of the Q-Tips with soap and jammed it into my dick. For three days I couldn't pee without tears welling in my eyes.

Mid—urethra swab, Debra pulled back the shower curtain.

"What kind of a fucking freak are you?"

Had it not been for the fact that a Q-Tip was dangling from the end of my dick, I might have had an answer for that. Instead, I said, "What are you doing in here?"

"I've got to take a crap."

I closed the shower curtain and put my head under the water, trying desperately hard not to listen as she shamelessly used the facilities a mere three feet away.

While I stood there, praying that my fecal encounter wouldn't lead to a hospital visit, I could swear I heard something like a grunt. I had lived my whole life in denial of the fact that women even had the capability of farting; reality as I understood it was crumbling.

It occurred to me that Debra and I probably weren't going to work out.

After that night I didn't give much thought to any sort of anal adventures. I spent the next year or two cautioning other men against such transgressions, telling them in excruciating detail my saga of coming head-to-head with the dreaded turtle.

I probably wouldn't have returned to the pleasures of the prostate had it not been for a phone sex conversation gone awry. At one point during our step-mother/step-son role-play, the "delectable milf" I had dialed said, "Oh, my sweet boy, I want you to let me fuck you in the ass with my big plastic dildo."

I came immediately, which was unfortunate since I had paid for twenty minutes.

After this, I became obsessed with finding a woman who would fuck me in the ass with a dildo. I would spend weeks and months testing the waters with various women, coaxing them to finger my ass while they gave me head. Those that made it that far (and they were an exclusive few) usually found one reason or another to conclude our relations for good when I asked them to entertain the thought of cornholing me.

Eventually, in a coffeehouse I frequented, I met Alice. She was an English major, and she had that dark, bohemian look that seemed to indicate that she was the type of girl who would fuck a guy in the ass, if only because it deconstructed traditional male/female relationships. I was not so idealistic that I wanted to hold out for a woman who was genuinely interested in buggering me, and if a few years of college had built up enough postmodern angst in a girl from the suburbs, I was entirely open to exploiting that.

I did not, however, anticipate falling in love with Alice. This complicated things because past experiences had taught me that not even a one-carat engagement ring could bind a woman so closely to me that she was willing to do that "dirty deed." Alice was also not interested in "toys." Whenever I suggested buying her a vibrator she dismissed the thought. When she introduced me to her parents several months into our relationship, I began to suspect that we were on a path of normality that barred the boinking of your boyfriend's butt. Things were getting out of hand. On the drive home from her parents' house, I finally said, "Look, do you love me?" She affirmed that this was the case. "Well, here's how it is..." And I related the tale of my mother's vibrator, of the ice cream scooper, even of the banana.

When I was done, Alice said nothing for a while. I was prepared to take her back to my place, let her collect her things and then bid her farewell so she could retreat to her friends and family with stories of what an absolute lunatic I was. Instead she said, "I think I have what you're looking for." The strap-on was black and made of rubber and was worn on a black leather harness. I marveled over it while Alice told me of her brief adventures on the Island of Lesbos.

I don't think I'd been as confused about the logistics of sex since I lost my virginity. We debated for some time the merits of me being face down, ass up; me on my back (because it's more romantic that way); both of us on our sides, spooning; or her lying back and me riding her. We settled with me being on my back.

I put a pillow under my ass and spread my legs. Alice was between them, the black dick dangling menacingly. She worked it over with K-Y and then pressed the head against my rear.

There are certain things that you forget while fantasizing, most notably that you are in complete control of a fantasy. When it comes down to things being "realized," you aren't in control at all, which is why when Alice pushed into me at what she felt was an acceptable rate, my eyes nearly shot out of my head. My own forays into my most forbidden of places had always been slow and gentle, and when I had relaxed a bit *then* I would speed things up. Years of exposure to overeager high school boys and drunken fraternity pledges (perhaps even exposure to *me)* had left Alice with the idea that one entered another with all the gusto of The Light Brigade galloping into the Valley of Death.

I began a hasty retreat up the bed but she stayed with me, and the rubber cock, which had appeared only slightly larger than my own member, was now an impossibly massive object lodged in my ass.

"Stop! Slow down!" I breathed.

Alice, who never spoke during our lovemaking, said, "You like it like this? You like this cock?"

I was mortified, if not because it felt like I had a softball in my butt, then because I felt things had turned ugly, and that any second now I would be compelled to put on my best Ned Beatty impersonation. I managed to say, "No!"

I wanted to say more, but Alice was going after me with rape-like intensity. I remember thinking something to the effect of, *But she's a woman! Doesn't she understand that no means no?*

Apparently she did not, which is why I drew my left leg back and kicked her in the head.

I did not offer an explanation, but instead fled once again to the shower, where all of these things seem to end up. I sat on the fiberglass floor of the shower and let the water cruise between my sore cheeks. I considered checking to see if I was bleeding, but I didn't really want to know. I didn't want this to finally be the time that my interest in the forbidden zone landed me in the emergency room.

Alice drew back the shower curtain with unrestrained authority.

"Do you want it or not?"

The cock waggled in my face as she spoke.

Before I could answer she said, "I mean, Jesus, Keck. It wasn't even all the way in yet."

My voice rose two octaves. "Not all the way in? What are you talking about?"

"I don't know," she said. "It felt like I was hitting something."

I said nothing. I drew back the shower curtain and waited until the water went cold.

Hard Evidence

I started masturbating when I was ten. I didn't get anything out of it, not so far as that divine nectar of the gods goes; mostly I just ended up with an irritated penis. I had devised a method of carving a hole in the center of a bar of soap and sliding my dick through it over and over. I had a much smaller penis then. After a few weeks of this my mother asked me why I was putting holes in the soap. I didn't touch myself again for two years.

After my rape of the Ivory (was it the soap's boastful claims to purity that I felt the instinctive need to sully?) and my recommencement of onanistic activity, I started feeling the need to enhance my "alone time" with a bit of theatrics. (It is a terrible curse to have been born on the cusp of that first generation lacking any shred of an attention span.) Things started out simply enough: a Victoria's Secret catalogue that I "borrowed" from the home of a neighbor, various sex manuals with helpful line drawings that my parents had closeted away from my curious adolescent eyes, the rare *High Society* magazine that I acquired in a trade for a Wade Boggs rookie card. I would close my eyes as my fist blazed a trail of passion up and down the shaft of my penis, imagining that those mute, two-dimensional beauties were right in front of me, begging for me to give them my hot load, and give it to them I did: I must have spilled my seed across the pages of thousands of centerfolds and lingerie models, sealing them shut forever, then burying them in the woods next to my parents' house so that my misdeeds would go undetected and I could avoid my mother's cross-examination: *Kevin, what are all these magazines doing under your mattress, and why do none of them open?* The humiliation of the "soap-hole inquisition" had stung me good, and I was resolved to avoid my mother's Gestapo-like prying into my penile affairs.

Of course, things escalated from the innocence of printed images. It wasn't long before I had discovered my father's stash of silent 8mm porn films (every young boy should have to try and load a reel of film with an insistent hard-on and fingers slick from Vaseline to develop a true appreciation for the internet). Moving from still photos to actual footage of people fucking was a personal victory that I equate with launching a dog into space: it was a small step in the right direction, but hardly the giant leap that my manhood had a hankering for. I wanted sound with my porn, heavy breathing and the *Oh Gods!* that I had read so much about in the plastered pages of the *Penthouse Forum*. Also, I wanted to dispense with the heavy machinery of 8mm erotica: nothing arouses as much curiosity in the ever-attuned ears of a mother as the sound of film projection equipment whirring away in her son's room at two in the morning.

I was eventually liberated by a copy of *Inside Seka* that my parents had borrowed on video from the next-door neighbors. Watching it was pure rapture: Seka was a blonde goddess, and after dealing with silent porn for so long, her orgasmic voice was a delight beyond compare. In one scene that was mildly moving, she phoned her husband and let him listen as she was entwined in a threesome. I watched that scene over and over, and at night when I couldn't risk the light from the television flickering in the dark house, I adjusted the controls so that the screen went black, and I lowered the volume and pressed my ear to the speaker as I roughed up my rod. Eventually the tape mysteriously vanished, most likely back to the neighbor's house, and I can only guess that it was the repeated viewing and listening of that scene in my youth which lead my in later years to turn to phone sex.

At first I called the pay services, but when I grew weary of party lines and bored operators, I knew I had to seek other answers. I turned to America Online, the best place in the world to go to find hot and willing girls who also have a fetish for auditory pleasures. A lot of the women I talked to just enjoyed listening as I stroked myself, but there was one girl I spoke to on a regular basis that had a mouth and mind like no other. She said she wanted me to fuck her in the ass, then come on her face. I wish to hell I knew what it is in a man's childhood that turns him on to facial shots. I don't remember Freud covering that one.

After one particularly memorable phone encounter, during which she implored me to take on the role of her father and punish her for doing bad things with her poodle (I never clarified if this was a euphemism or an actual dog), she said, "You know, I have a video of me playing with my pussy. Would you like to see it sometime?" I was overcome with such a sudden state of delirium that I felt the room begin to sway and pitch, and I panted an eager, "YES!" She said, "Ok, but you have to make me a tape of yourself and send it first."

I wasn't too keen on this. For one, I didn't have access to a camera on a convenient basis. Also, I didn't know if I could pull it off—it's bad enough when someone can see how foolishly maniacal you look during sex. I imagine most people look like village idiots while working themselves pretty good. With some hesitation I told her I would see what I could do, which was a complete fabrication. I had no intention of going through with it. Ever. Maybe at some point if I met this particular girl I would film myself *with her*, but that was the extent to which I was willing to document my flushed and naked body.

However, I have never really been a man of conviction, which is why shortly after her request, while on a visit to my parents' house, I decided to borrow their camcorder.

I set it up on the tripod, figured out where to aim it, and stripped down to nothing. As I prepared the little hog for the camera, shaking him from his flaccid slumber, I found myself without lubrication of any sort. Some men will swear by the comfort of their own pre-ejaculation and sweaty palm, but having rubbed myself to the point of drawing blood on more than one occasion, I had learned a little something about my own limits regarding friction. Besides, I have sensitive skin, and I regard my use of Vitamin E enriched lubricants as a way of not only protecting myself from the weathering agents of masturbation, but also as my way of "keeping it smooth for the ladies."

Unfortunately, on this trip home, I didn't bring my own lotion, and the only lotion I knew of was in my parents' room. I had tried too many times in my youth to steal into the folks' bed-chamber after they were asleep to plunder their supply of K-Y jelly, only to be thwarted by my mother's uncanny ability to sense when anyone was in her room. After some contemplation I visited the kitchen and spooned out a half-cup of butter flavored Crisco. I wondered for a moment if using such a cooking substance might alter the taste of my penis in some way, but I imagined this could only be for the better. I went back downstairs, greased my meat with vegetable shortening, and went to town on myself.

I was putting on a stellar performance, with some obligatory moaning going on (my off-camera moments of personal pleasure take place in relative silence, as I see no need to voice my satisfaction to myself). I was rubbing my balls with one hand, trying to take advantage of the full range of my skills. I contemplated fingering my asshole, but I thought that might be a bit much on my first tape. You have to save something for an encore. (My father taught me that, though I suppose my execution of his wisdom was pretty far from what he had in mind.) I made eye contact with the camera: I tried my best to look sexy, or at the very least not completely stupid. However, something had gone awry; the light that indicated the camera was recording had gone out.

I ceased with my endeavors and checked the machine. I decided the tape was screwed up and so I began to look for another one. My major problem with this whole affair was that since I was doing it on the fly I hadn't had time to buy a tape beforehand. The folks were all out of blanks and so I had merely grabbed one off of the top of the television. If there were something important on it, they would just have to deal with it. I found another tape marked *Perry Mason T.V. Movie* and quickly decided my dad would not miss Raymond Burr's later work.

The new tape worked fine. I got back in front of the camera and went to it. What the camera couldn't see was that I had dialed in the *Spice channel*. Some up-and-coming porn starlet was giving her all to Peter North. It was getting me in a very serious mindset about my task at hand, and I could feel the impending orgasm building in my balls. I scooted a little closer to the camera to let it go with my patented cry of, "I'm fucking coming!" I cleaned myself off, stopped the tape, and put it in for review. It was brilliant. I couldn't wait to send it out. I packed the camera back up and put the tape in my bag for my return trip to New York the next day.

Actually, it wasn't so brilliant. I mean, it was good, and I looked good. A lot better than I thought I would. But I was facing the camera. If you're a guy on film and you want your penis to look even remotely large, never face the camera: it doesn't capture the length. I shot a good load, and that looked hot— don't get me wrong. It's just that I was left feeling like I really hadn't captured the *real me*. Under the circumstances, though, it was good enough.

Still, after a few days, something was eating at me about the tape. I couldn't quite put my finger on it. I watched it a few more times, critiqued it a little more, and realized I bite my lower lip when I masturbate. Some women might actually find this attractive, but I thought I looked silly. Also, I had always felt a little insecure about the fact that when I masturbate I do it on my knees, and I've gotten nothing but grief about this when I share it with people. It's just how I feel most comfortable doing it. On tape it was rather charming. I guess you really have to see it for yourself to understand the mysterious beauty of my pose.

But I could never figure out what it was that kept popping up in my head like an ambiguous Mentos jingle. Then my mom called.

What I had forgotten about was the first tape that I had put into the video camera. I left it on top of the television. I never even glanced at what I had been recording over: *How to Use Your New IBM Computer*. Actually, had I taken a second to look at, I probably wouldn't have thought twice about using it. My parents had owned their computer for over a year. My grandfather, however, was a completely different story.

My mom and dad had gone to visit my grandparents to help them set up their new IBM computer. They took the tape. As I understand it, it didn't help my grandparents at all with using their computer. In fact, it left them rather puzzled.

When my mom told me all of this—over the phone,

sparing me the embarrassment of having to face her while evidence of my perversions was presented to me—I could feel my face turning red. Then, when she was done explaining how my father had nearly shit out his kidneys during the ordeal of trying to shut the tape off before my grandparents both succumbed to strokes, she said, "So, what do you have to say for yourself?"

What could I say? I had spent fifteen years of my life by this point trying to conceal a portion of my life that had suddenly been exposed in the most literal sense. I cleared my throat and said:

"I think I had the wrong camera angle. Did my wang look small?"

My mother paused, and then with nothing but supportive matriarchal affection said:

"Why, no honey, not at all."

I was a Teenage Homosexual!

So there I was, sixteen years old, with a fondness for The Cure and show tunes, not to mention the fact that I was regularly masturbating while prodding my rectum with a vast assemblage of household objects. On top of this, I had recently been exposed to *The Rocky Horror Picture Show* and had borrowed some of my mother's lipstick on a number of occasions to find just the right color for me. Of course, I told no one about these things. They were the dark secrets that I kept in my closet, and it was from this closet that I cleverly interpreted the obvious signs: I was what the other guys at school referred to as a "fucking faggot." I was not entirely happy with this terminology, and opted instead to quietly admit to myself that I was simply gay.

Granted, I was not terribly popular with the ladies at that age, which may have contributed to my assumption. When all of my friends were regaling me with tales of their experiments with girlfriends (wonderful stories that usually involved some type of fruit or public place), I simply nodded and tried to forget that most of my evenings were spent explaining my lengthy shower time to my parents. As if this weren't enough, I noticed a distinct lack of cock in late-night cable erotica. Too many times I caught myself thinking, This is all well and good, but I want to see a cock penetrating that woman and then coming on her. What truly heterosexual man longs to see a veritable chorus line of cocks ejaculating on a woman?

Then again, I never fantasized about having sex with a man, and I never watched gay porn (although I didn't have access to it even if I had wanted it — thanks to the Internet, the struggling gay adolescent has things much easier these days). But I did, quite by accident, end up masturbating in the dark with my friend Jeremy while we listened to Pink Floyd's "Several Small Species of Furry Creatures Gathered Together in a Cave and Grooving with a Pict," from the album *Ummagumma*.

We had been watching some ridiculous soft core porn that we rented from the local video store-- the basic plot seemed to involve competitive skiing-- I don't recall much more than that because we weren't interested in the plot and thus kept fast-forwarding from one lame sex scene to the next. When it was over, and our eager hormones had been sufficiently teased, I said something like, "Damn. I need to jack off."

How things proceeded from there is unclear, but I remember there was a small debate about whether or not I would really do it, then Jeremy said he would do it, then the lights were off, the music was on, and we moved to opposite sides of the room to begin our business.

To his credit, Jeremy was done almost immediately. And then he started again. This kind of pressure made it all the more difficult for me. Plus, because there was only one bottle of lotion between us, there was the constant interruption of passing it back and forth. And then there was the sound: in the dark, with Pink Floyd droning in the background, the sound of a greased fist vigorously working a cock could not be more absurd. When I finally got past that, Jeremy completely psyched me out by saying:

"Why do you hold your breath when you jerk off? You'll have a heart attack someday."

I had not been aware of my tendency to hold my breath while masturbating; still, there could have been few occasions more ill-suited for pointing this out. I was already feeling inadequate when faced with Jeremy's rapid fire ejaculation and recovery, and now I was being marked as a cardiac risk. It made me nervous that someone was paying such close attention to me as I masturbated. I told Jeremy to be quiet, and I turned up the music to drown out the sound of his activities and my respiration.

Forty-five minutes later, I finally finished. Jeremy was capping off his third of the evening. The next day, I told my mom that I wanted to get a perm.

The perm had a logic of its own. I had a terrible crush on the gay-and-permed fellow who choreographed the color guard for the marching band. Which, come to think of it, was another thing: I was in the color guard. I rarely admit to this detail of my life — to look someone in the eye and shamefully tell them that, instead of playing sports in high school, I chose to twirl a flag, is still a struggle.

Why I was attracted to this guy I can only venture to guess. He was charming and funny, as so many gay men seem to be. I was also charming and funny, and together we were a riot. Thus, our mutual charm and humor seemed yet another indicator of the fact that I was destined to suck cock.

Nothing ever came of my attraction to the color-guard choreographer, but secretly I started to reveal my sexual awakening to a few people, always women, because I felt they would be the least judgmental. Also, I was on the lookout for my requisite "fag hag." How could I be a bona fide homosexual without one? My confession would often happen late at night, toward the end of a party when I was alone with a girl on a porch, smoking a Virginia Slim and drinking the last of my wine cooler. I would sigh and say:

"You know, I think I'm gay."

Whatever girl I was with would go:

"Yeah, I knew that."

And that, more or less, was the end of it.

In the months following the initial self-abuse session between Jeremy and me, there were a few other instances that imitated the first one and Jeremy was always the champ during these marathon sessions. I surmised that this was why he did so well with the girls at school: he was never at a lack for a date, and his tales of sexual prowess were no secret. I personally bore witness to him having sex with a girl on the fire escape of a hotel fifteen minutes after meeting her, and then was dumbfounded with amazement as he nailed the prom queen less than an hour later.

As for me, my progress toward becoming a homosexual had reached a plateau. Although I was certainly the picture of a dandy as I fluffed out my perm at school every morning, I had yet to really be intimate with another man. Of course, I didn't give the matter much thought. I spent my hours in the shower thinking about women, but I knew this was just out of habit and that I would get over it soon.

By some good fortune I landed a copy of some really raunchy porn: lots of cocks, lots of cocks coming on women. I was delighted. Naturally, I extended an invitation to Jeremy to stop by that night. We took a ride out by the mall and picked up the new Cher album as a starter, after which we retired to the basement for a private screening.

Up until this point, Jeremy and I had always been shrouded in darkness when whacking ourselves. For the first time, in the light of the television, I saw his cock: it was a little misshapen, with an acute bend to the left at the tip. Jeremy had really launched into it once the porn got going, but I was having trouble keeping it up. We were sitting next to each other on the couch, and Jeremy reached over and took my cock in his hand and started stroking me. I was shocked; I had never felt another hand on my cock, and what was even more surprising was when I wrapped my hand around Jeremy's throbbing member: it was absolutely the strangest sensation, feeling this thing that was so familiar and yet completely alien. If this had been a woman, I would have been at a loss for what to do precisely, but I was certainly well-acquainted with the equipment, and so I began to move my hand up and down. Jeremy came in a matter of seconds. My own dong mustered a half-salute, then hunkered down and looked sullen. I remember feeling somewhat put off by the sensation of Jeremy's spunk on my hand.

I tried getting off on my own for about half an hour, during which time Jeremy jerked himself again. Finally I gave up, citing fatigue. That was the last time anything ever happened between Jeremy and me— or any other man. When my hair finally straightened out, I left it that way. I quit the color guard at some point, too. (It was a decision that prompted my father to give me $100 and remark, "Well, you've finally got your head on straight." There was not a hint of irony in his voice.) And in some fluke of fate I'll never understand, I ended up taking the homecoming queen to the prom and fucking her in the front seat of a friend's Dodge Daytona at a party later that night. I became incredibly drunk afterward and announced to those gathered around the keg, "Man, do I ever love that sweet, sweet pussy!" The homecoming queen never went out with me again.

Wet, Hot Presbyterian Summer

The day after I turned seventeen I was busted, along with some of my friends, for vandalizing a golf course in celebration of my existence. We had been under the influence of Milwaukee's Best Light, and while the damage to the course itself was relatively small, perhaps what was most embarrassing was having my parents informed of the theft of several back issues of *Penthouse* from the office of the greens keeper (my co-conspirators were quick to implicate me solely in that matter).

Instead of realizing that I was merely drunk, my parents concluded that wanton lust had bewitched me to the point that I needed serious help, and the only person capable of curing me was The Lord. (I might have tried to dispute this point more vigorously, but when I had returned home in the dismal hours of the early morning, my first act official act of being seventeen was to jack off over the pages of those *Penthouse*s while I leaned back on a broom handle that I had greased with Oil of Olay.) Since it was summer, my parents arranged to have me shipped to the mountains of North Carolina where I would be stationed at Camp Green, a retreat for the youth that needed to put themselves right with God.

When I arrived at the camp (on a Friday—the same day of the week as Jesus' crucifixion, let us not forget) I was more than shocked to find out that it was run by evangelical Presbyterians. At the time I was unaware such a hybrid of Southern bible thumping and New England restraint existed, and even more dismayed that my parents would turn me loose in their care for a month. After all, my parents were not entirely prudish people, and I suppose they were more upset by the public nature of my criminal activities than the crimes themselves.

During the orientation with all of the other campers and their parents, I noticed that there were a tremendous number of girls present who seemed to hint at the existence of a benevolent deity. I'd been primed with stories by friends of mine who had taken part in summer camp sexual experiments more heavenly than I could even begin to fathom, and their tales of pornographic archetypes—games of spin the bottle and truth or dare that tumbled madly into massive orgies, watching budding young girls shower together, soaping each other—suddenly filled me with a desire to stand in praise of God, which was unfortunate since I was wearing shorts with a propensity to "tent" excessively. This would not have been a problem had I been able to remain seated; as soon as my penis raised its head like a prairie dog scouting the grassy plains for predators, everyone was asked to stand and greet and get to know the people around him or her. I sat still for as long as possible until my father yanked me to my feet, then spun me around to face the most exquisite creature I had witnessed up until that point in my misguided life. She smiled, extended her hand, and when I reached out to take it she looked at my crotch, then twisted up her face in a way that suggested I had just presented her with a turd on a silver platter. I had just enough time to glimpse her nametag, which read "Lindsay Kapps" (the "i" was dotted with a heart) before she turned coldly away.

This event only added to my distaste for being squirreled away in the forest with people far more immersed in their faith than I, especially when Lindsay's retelling of our meeting made a rapid circulation of the camp gossip circuit. The sound of woodland creatures was often drowned out by the giggle of my Christian cohorts who were clearly not well versed in that whole "judge not lest ye be judged" bit. To make matters worse, one was never left alone—even traffic in the bathroom was constant—and before I knew it I had a gone a week without masturbating.

Perhaps this sounds like nothing more than a minor inconvenience, but as I was in the thick of my sexual prime it was more than just a setback: it felt as though the ripe sap of my loins was backing up into my brain and that very soon I would go mad. And as if it wasn't bad enough being under constant surveillance (because idle hands are indeed the devil's workshop), the boys and girls were separated throughout the day, so that the absence of the female form became a great weight that seemed clamped to my already weighty testicles. I longed so much to catch a glimpse of a tanned thigh with that light, downy hair settling upon it that my evening prayers developed a singular focus that I do not believe they were intended to have. I prayed for a woman's touch so intensely that I began to buy into all the camp propaganda: I *really* wanted to believe that God would answer my tortured cries for emancipation from the bondage of forced chastity.

For reasons I am unable to fully explain, at the outset of my second week I was given the chore of cleaning the bathhouses for the camp. It is my assumption that the camp counselor noticed my well-maintained bunk area and knew immediately that someone with my sanitary skills could be trusted to make the tile and porcelain sparkle. Or perhaps more accurately, my liberal use of the word "cocksucker" had placed me on someone's shit list.

I confess that the workings of my bowels are of great

interest to me, and pondering the size and frequency of my stools has helped me pass numerous hours in a pleasing manner. However, I have never cared for knowing what other people's bodies are capable of producing, let alone having to clean up after the production process.. My co-campers appeared to be youth of good breeding, but the amusement that they gained from not flushing the toilet, or stopping it up altogether with wads of toilet paper, told a different story: these people were filthy vermin. And it wasn't just the men. I had been sentenced to cleaning the women's restrooms as well, during the girls' lunch hour when their side of the camp was deserted.

My first day in their bathrooms was my first exposure to the hidden world or girls. I didn't like it, because I didn't like coming to terms with the fact that women crap. Or even the fact that women, too, seem to have difficulty flushing the toilet. And yet, despite all this, I was in heaven: I was finally alone.

In addition to toilets and showers, the bathhouses contained lockers (which didn't lock) in which we all stored our shower items. Each locker had a name on it, and I immediately found the one that belonged to Lindsay, the angelic beauty. Despite the fact that she had exposed me and given me the moniker "Rocket Man" (a title which was less flattering than it might sound), I still longed for her, and my cock pressed hard into my bunk at night as I lay there thinking about her.

I opened her locker, not exactly sure what I was looking for. Perhaps I thought some delicate of hers might have been left in there, or some sign of her own desires, but it was merely some soap, and some Pert shampoo. Without thinking, I unscrewed the shampoo bottle's lid and dumped a handful of Pert onto my cock and began stroking with

magnum force. Had I been able to keep up my regime of
masturbating a few times a day my experience might have
lasted longer, but even before I could begin to summon up a
suitable fantasy I felt myself coming, and before I could stop
myself I placed the open end of the shampoo bottle against
the head of my dick and let loose.

Many girlfriends have told me that when I ejaculate it's
quite a bit more than most other men they've been with.
Whether this is accurate or not I can't say, because I really
haven't invested a great deal of time exploring the matter,
but after ten days of not having an orgasm it felt like I
unloaded a gallon of jism into that shampoo bottle, and after
I came the odor of semen was more than apparent.
Naturally, I felt satisfied at first, and as I finished my
cleaning duties I felt rather smug. But I did feel a slight
twinge of guilt. After all, I had heard the urban legends of
vacationers who, having returned from their getaway to
paradise, find a few shots amongst their photos of hotel
clerks penetrating their rectums with the guests'
toothbrushes. Naturally, I had developed a healthy distrust
of housekeepers, and I always kept my toothbrush under lock
and key when I was away from home. And now, in my
moment of weakness, hadn't I become as deplorable as those
deranged individuals? Hadn't I committed some vile sin,
made all the worse by the fact that I was among God's
people, learning to do God's good work?

I went through the rest of the day wracked with guilt, but
I was distracted later that night by some very intensive
square dancing (an activity that becomes surprisingly erotic
in the absence of any other sexual outlet), and by the time I
went to sleep I had forgotten all about my handy-work in the
girls' lavatory. When I woke up, and my penis was shedding
its skin like a serpent, I had no trouble recalling what act had

visited this pestilence upon me. I have never been so terrorized upon awakening as I was that morning: in the space of a few hours my prick had gone from a silky whiteness to a rough and leathery brown; the head was puffy and red—it looked angry, and very much like a polish sausage that had been forgotten under the heat lamps for a fortnight. It was clear to me that God was pissed, and that this was the burden I would have to bear for my sins. I was like Job, but my pox was of a more private nature.

All that day my cock was terribly painful to touch, and each time I peed it felt as though the very fires of hell with licking at the tip of my penis. In addition to this, it itched more fiercely than the chigger bites which I had suffered on my inner thighs my first week in camp, so now was I not only the boy who popped wood at the mere prospect of a handshake, I was also the boy who couldn't cease tugging at his crotch. When I was afforded the luxury of being alone during my cleaning duties, I peeled huge strips of skin off of my penis, leaving it red and raw. After two days of this I couldn't take it anymore. My prayers miraculously lost their theme of camper copulation and moved instead toward genuine begging forgiveness. When I woke on the third day, I was healed: my cock was more smooth to the touch than ever. It looked amazingly purified; it practically glowed.

I turned over a new leaf. I became the model camper, and I didn't touch myself again until I had returned home. In fact, in those remaining weeks at camp I became somewhat of a role model, even earning the award at the end of the month for the "Most Improved Attitude," an award about which I was disturbingly prideful.

On the last night at camp we had a rather moving service, during which I expounded to my peers about my sinful past, and how in this month away from the world I had been touched by the Holy Spirit (leaving out the specifics, of course). After the service, when we were finally allowed to freely mingle, I found myself down at the dock, alone with Lindsay, the object of my undying affection. In the moonlight, her hair had a healthy sheen to it, and I silently took credit for that. When she leaned into kiss me, I turned away: I told her I wasn't the man she thought I was, and that I was following God's path now. She nodded in understanding, and we walked quietly back to where the other were.

When I returned home, I avoided my friends—I just didn't think there was a place for them in my new life, my life of service to The Lord. I finally did break down and go to party with them, but only so that I could act as the designated driver—I explained it was only my concern for their well being which allowed me to cavort with such sinners. While at the party I became involved in a conversation with a rather flamboyant Malaysian fellow who was narrating his recent experience of being gay bashed. I expressed sympathy and shock, which he casually dismissed with a wave of his limp wrist:

"Oh, honey," he said, "don't sweat it. All those meaty white jocks pounding me got me so hot that when I finally got up off the street I went in the bushes and jacked off. It's just a damn shame it hurt so much."

"Did they rack your balls that badly?" I asked, stunned that any man, gay or straight, would ever inflict that kind of harm on another man.

"Oh, no. They didn't touch me there," he said, sounding vaguely disappointed. "I'd beat off with some Pert shampoo two nights before, and that stuff had peeled the skin right off my dick. Shit. You talk about *raw*."

I felt the blood drain from my face, and it became more

than evident that there was a God, and that not even he was on my side.

Delicates

The Summer I was thirteen, my neighbors paid me twenty bucks to feed their dog and collect the mail while they were away for a week. They gave me a key to their house, and they hadn't been out of the driveway for five minutes before I was in the master bedroom, rummaging through the wife's underwear drawer.

The precise neurological impulse that caused me to do this remains a mystery, although I'm pretty sure it was connected to the fairly recent discovery that I could masturbate happily for hours. I was constantly on alert for all things sexual, and even though I was young, I understood that for most people, sexuality was something kept hidden in drawers, in the tops of closets, and under the bathroom cabinet.

This was where my parents hid their own variety of Freudian interests, which included a cock ring nestled in a brown bag, along with some clothespins and a feather boa. Before my penis began pressuring me into mildly criminal behavior (North Carolina has a viciously strict series of sex laws, and I am certain they forbid the soiling of undergarments belonging to another man's wife), I spent hours covertly going through my parents' stuff, combing their bedroom for clues to the mystery of mating.

Had my mother and father actually been as boring as they appeared, my life might have taken a different route. As it stands, they apparently liked to fuck as much as the next couple, so I unearthed a wealth of porn films, magazines and instructional pamphlets. I never confronted my parents with my findings, but I grew increasingly skeptical about whatever "truths" they had to tell me. They had burned me once with the whole Santa Claus debacle, and I wasn't going to allow myself to be duped like that again. I was convinced that my parents, along with every other adult in my neighborhood, were keeping something from me.

Excavating my neighbors' bedroom only substantiated my hypothesis. The husband had a treasure trove of Playboys — every issue going back ten years. So for the length of their vacation, my sole interest in life was to be in their house, masturbating to whatever beauty that Hugh Hefner had crowned for a month's reign.

However thrilling as the naked pictures were, I kept being lured back to the underwear drawer of the wife, Gina. She was a young mother, in her late twenties, and she had a way of interacting with people that hinted she was a sensual creature. Whenever she touched me, I felt a mixture of discomfort and excitement.

Her drawer was a cornucopia of undergarment fashion, running from standard cotton whites to a pair of crotchless red lace. Not being terribly familiar with women's underwear on a one-to-one basis, the reason for such panties' existence completely eluded me at the time. My first thought was that this variety of underwear was designed to allow hassle-free urination in real clutch situations. After all, my mother would complain about the length of the women's restroom line whenever we went someplace public, so I could imagine instances where speed was a valued commodity.

I took off my shorts and stepped into the crotchless red panties, putting them on over my white briefs. Their purpose became immediately self-evident. I looked at myself in the mirror: a thin, thirteen-year-old boy in briefs and red lace crotchless panties. I didn't feel strange seeing myself like

that, and that fact — along with the purchase of an Amy
Grant album in 1990 — haunts me to this day.

The afternoon before my neighbors returned, I dumped
all of Gina's underwear out on the bed and rolled around
naked in it, stroking myself. I was careful to put everything
back in a way that revealed as little as possible, but
nonetheless, that was the only time I was ever asked to
house-sit. For years, I thought nothing of it, until I realized
that I had been quite liberal with their petroleum jelly and
lotion, and that I always cleaned up with their towels, then
disposed of them in the laundry hamper without washing
them.

For years after my week in the Xanadu of my neighbors'
house, I didn't have many opportunities to ravish unattended
lingerie. On the few occasions when I did have unrestricted
access to various apartments and houses, it was usually for
the purposes of pet-sitting, and the delicates in question
either belonged to grandmotherly types or women who held
no allure for me.

When I was a senior in high school, I broke down and
asked my girlfriend for a pair of panties. To my surprise, she
readily consented. But when I was alone with my bounty at
the end of the night, I found myself totally uninterested in
what I had coveted for so long. A week after she gave them to
me, I was at her house swimming. When I went inside to use
the bathroom, I slipped into her older sister's room, shut the
door behind me, found her underwear drawer, knelt before it
and masturbated. (It was fortunate that the drawer's height
was simpatico with my peculiar necessity to be on my knees
while I flog myself).

I came in less than thirty seconds, then realized, after the
fact, that I had soiled several of her panties. It would have
been too risky to throw them all in the laundry, so I mixed

things up in the drawer a bit. That seemed to make the scene of the crime look more or less normal, but the drawer's contents still smelled like come. I swore that if I didn't get caught, I would never violate a woman's space like that again.

I kept that promise until I was in grad school. My upstairs neighbor, Holly, was the most heavenly of all God's creatures, and although she and I became good friends, that's all it was ever going to be. I knew this because she told me, "Keck, I would never fuck you. I just couldn't take it seriously." I had heard that before, and prior experience had prepared me for spending weekends with the object of my affection while she pined away for one joker or another.

I don't know why I snapped with Holly. I suppose it had to do with her taking a shower while I was sitting in her apartment watching *Under Siege 2*. On the way to the bathroom, she walked past the living room and told me to make myself comfortable; she was only wearing a towel, and I could see the double crescent of her ass peeking from under the hem.

After I suspected Holly was in the shower and unlikely to know what I was doing, my first instinct was to fall to my knees and masturbate. There was a bottle of lotion on the coffee table, a roll of paper towels by the television. Every single prop I needed was in place, and for some reason I stopped. I stood up, walked to the bathroom door, listened for her movements. Then I went back down the hallway to Holly's bedroom.

My hands were shaking as I opened and closed her drawers, searching for the right one. (Naturally, it was the last one I opened.) The first thing I saw was a pair of undies with a fruit print. I started to grab those but hesitated; clearly they were atypical. The rest of the drawer held standard black lace, cotton whites, some tasteful and understated designer numbers. I was somewhat disappointed, but that didn't change the fact that I had a tremendous, throbbing erection.

Suddenly I couldn't hear the shower running. I grabbed a pair of beige Calvin Klein's and headed back to the TV. Just as I reached the hallway and was stuffing her panties into my pocket, the bathroom door opened. I stopped in my tracks and turned to the wall, facing a poster that was one of those 3-D puzzles that one has to solve by going cross-eyed.

"What are you doing?"

I didn't answer her right away, trying instead to get my breathing under control. I focused intensely on the eye puzzle.

"I'm trying to solve this puzzle," I said.

"Haven't you already done that?"

I had already solved it, the very first night I had ever been in her apartment. She had caught me red-handed.

"Oh, right," I blurted. "Well, actually, I heard the shower stop, and I was waiting for you to come out, because I need to take a leak."

I pushed past Holly and into her bathroom without waiting for a response.

Once I was in the bathroom, I leaned back against the door and steadied myself. My right hand was still thrust in my pocket, disguising the bulge of wadded-up underwear. They appeared to be some sort of polyester blend — definitely not silk, but still marginally sexy to the touch. Without thinking, I fell to my knees, took out my cock, wrapped the underwear around it, and made perhaps six full strokes before I came all over them.

It wasn't until that particular moment that I fully considered the consequences of my actions: I had transgressed against the cosmos by failing to abstain from defiling other people's underwear. I was going to pay, and I knew that the impending calamity would be brutal in its scope.

I had to try and reverse my actions, make things right with the world. I quickly resolved that I would wash the underwear, and then just as stealthily as I had ganked the Calvin's, I would return them to their rightful place. No harm, no foul.

I stuffed the sticky panties in my pocket and left the bathroom. Holly called out from her bedroom:

"Come back here and tell me how this skirt looks." Because she had been candid about the fact that we would never copulate, Holly somehow thought that I wouldn't lie to her about how she looked. (Apparently because there was no ultimate payoff for me.)

She was standing in her walk-in closet, looking in the mirror.

"Well?" she said.

I looked her up and down. Then, I noticed them: Lying at her feet was a pair of black underwear that hadn't made it into her clothes hamper. My heart began to palpitate. I had never gotten my hands on panties that were fresh from the field. Since I had made an arrangement with my conscience to right my early wrongs, I decided that another pair wouldn't hurt.

"I don't know. It seems a bit tight. Can you move freely in it?"

"I guess so."

"There's no time for guessing, Holly. There's nothing more silly-looking than a girl who's bound too tightly in her skirt. Walk to the end of the hallway and back to be sure."

My reasoning was absurd, but Holly was just insecure

enough to buy it. She left her bedroom, taking longer strides than usual. I pounced on the panties lying in the closet and plunged them into my vacant pocket. When she returned, I was standing casually by the bed, examining a copy of *Self.*

"You're right," she said. "It is too tight."

When I was finally alone in my own apartment, I closed all the blinds and pressed Holly's worn panties to my face. They smelled musky. I examined them closely: the crotch held the unmistakable residue of dried vaginal secretions. Oh, it was too much! I was delirious, and for a second time that night I fell to my knees and masturbated. This time, however, I pressed the scented underwear to my face, while my first catch of the evening bore witness to a second coming. When I finished, I pledged to swear off women's underwear. I placed the profaned panties in the bottom drawer of my nightstand and forgot about them for a month.

My apathy in returning Holly's underwear was, more or less, due to my inability to figure out a way to replace them without being caught. I had read enough Agatha Christie in my youth to know that criminals are often apprehended when returning to the scene of the crime. I finally realized what I had to do: wait until she put a load of laundry in the washer (which was in the basement of our building), slip in after she had gone back to her apartment, and put her underwear in the wash. That's precisely what I did. I surmised that Holly would be none the wiser, and all would be right with the universe.

After I made the drop-off, I sat in my apartment, relieved that I had finally rid myself of the horrible albatross of Holly's underwear. I was certain that I had desecrated my last piece of ladies' apparel, and I was grateful to whatever forces of nature allowed me to escape discovery. Then came the knock on my door.

When I opened it, Holly was standing there, and she thrust the evidence of my betrayal in my face. I was mortified.

"The most fucked-up thing just happened!" she said. "I've been missing these panties for weeks. I mean, I've been looking for them everywhere, because they go with two of my favorite bras, and when I took my laundry out, there they were. What the fuck do you make of that?"

I studied her face; she didn't seem accusatory, just genuinely puzzled.

"It must be static cling," I said. "It is winter."

Holly seemed relieved by this, as if she had imagined that some creep was invading her laundry and having his way with her delicates. She started up the stairs toward her apartment, and I pretended not to notice that a thong was about to slip from her laundry basket.

Stranger than Friction

I'd quietly been denying for months that something was
wrong — *bad wrong* — with my wiener. The problem was
that it was beginning to look just like an actual wiener — not
the smooth, fresh, glistening Ball Park frank that causes one
to salivate even before you've slipped it from the package and
onto the grill, but that off-brand hot dog of dubious origins
that becomes wrinkled and leathery if microwaved for too
long.

Most men would have carted themselves down to the
emergency room at the first sign of an affliction like mine,
but my penis had endured plagues far worse than this. As an
adolescent, I once made the mistake of masturbating with
Pert shampoo and then watched with horror as my wang
shed its skin for three days. Fortunately, my terror turned to
delight when my member ultimately emerged as immaculate
as it was in my infancy — only bigger. Once you've seen that
— and admittedly, it happened more than once; I'm not very
quick when it comes to cause/effect relationships — it takes
something more than a weird little dermatological problem
to spur you toward the assistance of a medical professional.

But then came the spots, itchy and inflamed. What's
worse, it felt goddamned great to scratch them. Soon, no
woman would come within twenty yards of my raw, exposed
member. I couldn't blame them — I wanted to distance
myself from the diseased dick as well.

At the onset of my condition, I was still dating a woman
named Marissa. I managed to conceal things from her pretty
easily. Because I'm not overly fond of blowjobs, most of our
sexual activity took place in areas that were lit

"romantically." One evening, though, I stepped out of the shower while Marissa was in the bathroom. She grabbed my dick and squatted before me, then looked up with alarm. "What the fuck? Is this normal?"

"Yes. I think the stubble from your bikini line irritated me somehow."

Marissa held my penis in her hand for a moment, staring at it like a ceramics project gone awry. Then she said, "No. Nope," stood up, and walked back into the bedroom. Her phone calls dwindled after that. I spent many lonely hours trying to convince myself it was coincidence.

Simply put, my fear of doctors prevailed over my fear of my penis turning black and falling off. I believed that things would simply clear up within a few weeks. Of course, "things" didn't clear up, but only varied in intensity and type.

At the doctor's office, a young receptionist with red hair and excellent dental coverage smiled at me while updating my insurance information. I shamelessly gawked at her cleavage as I accepted the paperwork.

"You look very healthy," she said. When I assured her that I *was* quite healthy, she smiled some more.

When my doctor came into the examination room, he looked as though he was in a tremendous hurry. Most of our previous meetings had been brief, with an exam and a prescription delivered in less than five minutes. Before I could even begin to tell him my troubles, he said, "I've been on call all week, and I can't even tell if I'm still awake. These assholes at the nursing home are killing me." He pursed his lips and produced a lukewarm smile. "So what's up with you?"

I took a moment to collect myself, exhaled deeply, then stood up and walked across the room toward the door. When I reached it, I turned around and went back to the examination table.

The doctor raised his eyebrows.

"Did you hear that?" I asked.

"Yes," he said. "Is that coming from where I think it is?"

"Yes."

"How long?"

"For a while now."

He pursed his lips again and made a small praying motion with his hands. "Well, you're getting older. Your knees and ankles will begin to pop like that, especially if you're sedentary. Get some more exercise. How's everything else? You look a little pale." He began to feel my glands and take my pulse.

"Everything else is good," I said. "Real good. Well, there was one thing I was wondering about. I've got this. . . I don't know . . . rash."

He frowned and began to wash his hands without saying a word. While the doctor turned his back to retrieve a pair of latex gloves, I unbuckled my belt and dropped my pants. I was nervous, and the room was cold: there were few combinations more ill-suited for baring one's penis. I imagined my doctor going home to his wife that night and saying, "You should have seen it today, honey! That older Keck boy has a penis like a peanut!" He was only my doctor, but I didn't want to go down in his personal lore as the man with the curiously shrunken dick. In the place where I live, things like this have a way of making themselves public: notes on charts fall under the eyes of chatty medical assistants, and suddenly every one in town knows that Skip Edwards has only one testicle. I'd also heard horror stories from friends who had gone for ambiguous tests: cotton swabs attached to long metal rods plunged into the urethra, tissue samples snipped from the foreskin. There was no way this could have a happy ending.

When my physician turned around, he stared at my groin and said:

"Good lord."

Normally, I'm delighted with this type of reaction. I have a tall and thin build, and people seem to expect my penis to reflect my delicate stature. However, the doctor's face didn't relay admiration. In fact, it didn't even register as being the face of a calm, indifferent medical professional. It bore a look of genuine horror.

After he snapped on his gloves, the doctor kneeled and grabbed my dick as if it were a fraternity brother he hadn't seen in twenty years. He squeezed and pinched my testicles and shaft for several seconds, then took a bit of foreskin between his index finger and thumb and held my rod as though it were a dead mouse his cat had left on the doorstep. With his free hand, the doctor poked a few areas, then let my damaged dick drop back into its preferred left-leaning hang.

He shook his head. "What the hell did you do to this thing?"

It was the first time I had heard a physician refer to a portion of my anatomy in the same manner someone might address a mangled used car. "Nothing out of the ordinary," I said, though his look indicated that I had done something quite extraordinary.

"What do you masturbate with?" He had a notepad out and was poised for my answer.

"My hand." I thought this was fairly obvious, but recalling several experiences with child-safety flotation devices in my teenage years, I understood the necessity of his question.

The doctor shook his head again. "No, what sort of lubrication do you use? Anything unnatural?"

And here I pulled my pants back on, cleared my throat

and looked shamefully at the floor as I recounted nearly eighteen years' worth of the various products applied to my penis. Vaseline, lotions of all sorts, K-Y Jelly, baby oil — these items didn't even cause the good doctor to raise an eyebrow. It was when I rattled off the litany of shampoos and soaps, cooking oil, motor oil, 3-in-1 oil, toothpaste, Neosporin, Smuckers Apple Jelly, Vicks VapoRub, Papa John's garlic-butter sauce, Chapstick, sunblock, Hawaiian Tropic Tanning Oil, Old Spice, butter, and margarine (for what it's worth, margarine most definitely holds up better than butter). Many of these items I used more than once, but the ice cream resulted in such a catastrophic mess that I must strongly discourage its use.

When I was finished, the doctor merely looked at me and blinked. I looked away and tried to imagine what med-school course could have prepared him for this.

Seconds passed in silence. "Don't touch yourself for three weeks," he said. "Never use anything but Vaseline or K-Y when you do masturbate, and consider yourself lucky."

"Lucky?" My voice rose to a falsetto.

The doctor rubbed the bridge of his nose in a manner I found painfully familiar. I often did the same thing when I was forced to explain something quite simple to one of my particularly dense students. "Do you remember what you just told me? You've put chemicals that were meant for *automobiles and cooking* on the most sensitive part of your body. When you die, you should have it cut off and sent to a research lab."

It was what I always wanted to hear: my penis was a marvel fit for serious scholarly research. But it was a bittersweet revelation. My little man would end up in the mason jar reserved for freakish wonders, not the decanter marked "Huge Discovery." It was more likely to find its way

into the gawkish halls of a *Ripley's Believe It or Not!*
museum than the Smithsonian.

I gave serious thought to the urges that often sent me to
my knees, my palm slick with whatever lubricating substance
was most conveniently at hand. It occurred to me that all of
my recent visits to the doctor had involved either my head or
my butt. (My family has an unfortunate genetic inclination
toward depression on one side and hemorrhoids on the
other.) And now, my genitals.

"Look," my doctor was saying. "Can you do that? Can you
just not touch it? Just don't touch it. It's that simple. You're a
grown man. Don't. If it isn't looking better in two weeks, call
me, but just . . . just don't." He shook his head, peeled off his
gloves and walked out of the room.

As I left, I stopped at the receptionist's desk to pay. My
chart lay open in front of her. The doctor's handwriting was
not as illegible as I would have liked, and his diagnosis —
penis excoriated from masturbation — stood out on the page
like a marquee advertising my shame.

When I handed the receptionist a check, she didn't even
crack a smile.

54

Cherry Picker

I once went on a date with a woman who told me that at the age of eighteen she lost her virginity to a man who was an actual Tantric Master. Up until that point the evening had been sailing along magically, and beneath our conversation I could hear a choir of seraphim singing hallelujahs and other such praises to Eros. Of course, after the narrative of the tantric master ended, the choir of angels became a barbershop quartet of insecurity. The revelation that my date lost her virginity to a tantric master is a little like cooking her dinner and then finding out that her father is one of the premiere chefs of France: it's hard to feel anything but a little defeated.

The loss of my own virginity was simply that: a loss. On the brighter side, it was such an utter disappointment that every other sexual encounter I've had since has seemed rather transcendental by comparison. It might not have been such an anticlimactic experience (and sadly, it *did* lack a climax) had I actually been the first choice of the lady I ended up—very literally—rolling in the hay with.

I met her at a party when I was just barely sixteen. I had been watching her all night; she was a southern, white trash vixen, and while that may seem a derogatory remark to some, those of you from above the Mason and Dixon and west of the Mississippi must accept as gospel my assertion that a steady diet of grits and fatback through your youth instills in one an insatiable desire for cutoff jeans and big hair. My friend, Johnny Mason, had spent his evening making out with her against the side of R.J. Ryder's house,

unzipping her cut-offs and playing with her pussy. I know
this because I watched it take place from the vantage point of
the keg, which offered a beautiful locale from which to view
the vista of teenage gropings taking place all around. When
Johnny finally ducked around to the other side of the house
to puke, the girl whose teased hair that had been calling to
me all night slouched against the wall and looked bored. I
sauntered over and smoothly said:
    "Cool party."
    "Yeah," she said, not looking at me as she put a Marlboro
in her mouth. It had not been too many weeks before that my
father had taken me aside and imparted upon me what he
felt to be great wisdom:
    "Boy, just you remember: a woman who will smoke a
cigarette will do just about anything."
    I thought about this for a second and said:
    "Didn't mom used to smoke?"
    "Used to," he mumbled, and seemed to be momentarily
overcome by wistful memories I cannot begin to guess about.
    As I was debating the accuracy of my father's advice,
Johnny stumbled back around the corner and said:
    "I'm fucked up." Few words have ever sounded sweeter,
for I knew at that moment that Johnny was out of the
picture. As he weaved away from us and towards his car, his
abandoned nymph turned to me and said:
    "Walk me down to the woods so I can take a piss."
    I followed her down to edge of the woods, not saying too
much, and when she thrust her beer into my hand and
squatted to urinate right in front of me I politely turned
around. When she finished she said:
    "Let's lay here in the grass for a while."
    Being fairly inexperienced with women at this phase in
my life I was utterly mortified. I lay stiffly next to her, not

moving, until she pulled me on top of her and started kissing me. After a few minutes of this she unzipped my pants and asked:

"Do you love me?"

That was the first instance of a woman touching my penis on purpose. Up until that point I had masturbated profusely to the time when Barbie Watson had accidentally brushed against my over-excited member during a dance. The sudden sensation of a hand other than mine on my dick was overwhelming. Had she asked me if I desired to be drawn and quartered while fire ants were funneled into my rectum I would have gasped, *Yes! Anything! Oh, anything you want, just please never let go!*

Which is precisely what I meant when I looked into her eyes and said:

"Of course I love you." And at that, she pulled back her panties, and slid me into her.

Prior to actually engaging in intercourse, I was convinced that sex must be the adult equivalent of Disney World. Masturbation seemed pretty close to magical on certain occasions, but the looks on the faces of the porn stars, and the way premarital sex was forbidden by most major religions, gave me the sense that sex with another person unlocked secrets that bound the very fabric of the cosmos together. I mean, why else would people get so excited about it? It couldn't just be because it felt good. Plenty of things *felt* good, and a lot of those things were not only allowed, they were even encouraged.

Instead of swooning into an intercourse induced delirium, as I suspected I would when I first made contact with the long sought after beaver, my mind did a curious thing that it has done frequently during sexual activity since: it kind of wandered. I couldn't focus on the lass who was spreading her legs to cure me of my innocence. I was too busy analyzing what was going on, entertaining such thoughts as: *Is this girl really pretty, or am I just horny? Also, the vagina seems to sit kind of low...* (For some reason, my observation of porn and inexperience with female anatomy had me thinking that the vaginal opening was about an inch or two higher than it was; it seems a trivial observation now, but at the time it was rather rattling). And the thought that perhaps kept me from slipping into splendor the most: *Damn. I'm getting laid in the middle of a field at a keg party. I wonder if anyone is watching?*

Never mind the standard insecurities that accompany anyone on their first sexual encounter, as soon as it dawned on me that I might be putting on a show for the drunken mob, I couldn't even approach being interested in what was going on. I poked my head up and looked around: we were about thirty yards away from the party where it was somewhat shadowy; no one seemed to be paying attention. I imagined that in the darkened area where we lay it was probably hard for anyone to really see what was going on, even if they could get a glimpse of our darkened forms in the cloak of the late Spring night.

Then I was fucking in a spotlight.

At first I wasn't sure what was going on. It did occur to me that I might have had too much to drink, that I might have wandered into the house and passed out in someone's bed, and that this was the end of the dream: the flood of overhead light stirring me from my slumber mixes momentarily with the dream world, and I am briefly suspended between the two, bathed in 60 watt light and alone, but still humping away in my anxious brain so that it feels like I am center ring at a surreal sexual circus.

But I had nothing to drink that night, which was out of

the ordinary for me. And I *was* having sex, which was also
out of the ordinary for me. I looked up and realized that
some asshole had turned the headlights of his car on,
illuminating me as my unpracticed hips struggled to
maintain an unfamiliar rhythm. I felt my dick begin to lose
its solid strength; relocation was in order.

"Hey babe," I breathed, "why don't we go into the woods
over there?"

"I'm fine here," she said dreamily.

I wasn't prepared for her response. The way in which all
of this had transpired seemed to happen so easily that I
thought surely this girl would cater to my every whim. I felt
that maybe she needed to know the reason, so I said:

"Some people have their headlights on watching us."

"Cool."

I would not be shaken in the least at this point in my life
if my partner wanted me to participate in putting on a show
for total strangers. I'm certain I would find it to be pretty hot,
but losing your virginity to a girl you just met, and in the
middle of a field outside at a party, and then to top that off
by making it a public performance... it was just more than I
could handle. I pulled out, stood up, pulled her to her feet,
and lead her to the woods. As she bobbled along behind me
she said, "I'm hungry... Is there any food?"

It was obvious to me that my unskilled labors of love
impressed the young lady almost as much as if I had gone
into an impromptu recitation of Wordsworth. She dutifully
lay down on a mulch pile once we were in the woods, spread
her legs and beckoned me to finish up.

Unfortunately, my own neuroses about my performance
were becoming insurmountable odds by that point, and as I
pressed my limp dick pointlessly against her unyielding
vagina, I thought that maybe I might be cured of my first

bout with impotence by receiving my first blowjob. Of course, the only experience I had with coaxing a woman to put her mouth around one's penis came from adult films. And so, with a certain panache that shames me to this day, I looked my accomplice in the eye and asked, "Are you still hungry?"

"Yeah," she said naively.

"Well, how would you like a hot dog?" And with that, I flung my limp member in front of her face. She let out a quick, "Ha!" However, her exclamation did not carry a note of amusement, but rather the disappointed tone of a girl who has sobered up just enough to realize she has offered up her pussy to a total moron.

She took my cock in her mouth, toked on it a few times with little success, and without speaking we both seemed to reach a point where the ordeal seemed better off coming to an end. I stood up and dusted the mulch from my knees, she shook it from her underwear, and we walked back into the field and towards the party that did not seem to have realized our absence.

"Well, okay..." and I trailed off.

"Yeah," she said. "I'm going to..."

"That's cool, that's cool." We weren't looking at each other.

"Okay." And with that we parted.

When I found my friends at the party and told them I had gotten laid, *finally*, they could not have cared less. Instead, J.B. said to me, "If you didn't have my car keys I was gonna leave your ass here."

The next day at school I overhead Trina Bonner saying, "... and I heard she fucked this guy in the woods, and then she fucked like five more dudes after that in the house." I thought at first that this was another girl, but there was no

denying it was my own sweet nymph that had made me a
man. For a while I comforted myself with the thought that I
had been good enough to whet her appetite that night, but
then I came to the conclusion that there is no pride in being
an appetizer.

In the next three years I would have sex with four other
women, and the total number of times I engaged in
intercourse in those three years would be eight. While at
least two of those encounters had been the stuff that a young
boy's masturbation fantasies are made of, none of them
prepared me to deflower my first long-term girlfriend, Leslie.
    Like Nabokov's ill-fated Humbert and Lolita, my pursuit
of Leslie's maidenhead extended over such a long period
time, and had to surmount so many obstacles, by the time we
found ourselves ready to copulate in my parents' basement
on my twentieth birthday we were doomed.
    Leslie was younger than I, just sixteen, and like a lot of
sixteen year-old girls she changed her mind a lot. What she
changed her mind about most was me. It seemed that in the
year leading up to our eventual union, each time our level of
intimacy reached a new plateau, she dumped me. When
three months of heavy kissing and petting gave way to a
hand job, I got a few of those and then she dumped me. I
pined away for a month, then she came back, gave me
blowjobs for a while, then dumped me again. Invariably,
what I discovered was that I was a sort of guinea pig for her
sexual exploration. Once she felt comfortable with whatever
new sexual act she had added to her arsenal, I was of no
more use to her. She then went back into the world to use her
charms on more desirable boys. My grasp of this pattern was
solid enough by my twentieth birthday that I knew whatever

boinking I got to do with Leslie would be fleeting.

My parents were comfortable with my girlfriends sleeping over at our house as long as we shared separate beds. Of course, any parent who thinks their child might abide by this rule after the onset of hormones must be living in a cave, but not a cave that has any Freudian meaning.

After my parents had retired for the night I snuck downstairs to where Leslie lie in bed waiting for me. From the moment I entered the room I had a sense that something special was afoot: the smell of Victoria's Secret lotion hung heavy in the air. When we had worked ourselves into a good lather, which took as little time as you might expect, I positioned myself to enter Leslie.

She wisely requested that I use a condom, and like many men, I felt my penis begin to shrink from such a thought. I can't fathom why it is that putting on a condom can cause a rigid penis to collapse with lightening speed, but I would wager it's something similar to finding out you have won a free back massage, and then finding out that you have to receive the massage while wrapped in an oriental rug.

When I had finally unrolled the condom onto my flaccid penis, and then coaxed the penis to an erection again and pressed the head against Leslie's moist center, she stopped me.

"I can't do this without music."

I understood: the only sound was the sound of our bodies, and the music would somehow ease the weight of the circumstances. I turned on the clock-radio to a jazz station, and the romantic melodies of fingers tickling a piano swelled into the room.

"This sucks," Leslie said. "Put it on the Top 40 station."

I wasn't about to argue with her. If she wanted pop, she could have pop; all I wanted was that elusive vagina of hers that I had dreamed of for over a year. I had beat myself senseless imagining how she would enfold me like a velvet envelope, how her face would look as I entered her, how she would sound coming, how she would look with my come on her. I was prepared to give her whatever she wanted.

I wasn't prepared to wait for another hour as she deemed one song after another inappropriate or unworthy of this, her first time. I kept having to keep myself hard, in a condom no less, and when I finally ripped it from jerking too hard, I had to go through the minimizing ordeal of putting another one on, lest Leslie call me into action at any moment.

When Tom Cochran's "Life is a Highway" finally wafted over the airwaves, Leslie was ready. Urban legends had primed us both for Leslie being in pain when I entered her for the first time; experience has taught me that adequate lubrication can make many things utterly painless. As I pressed into her she winced: I drew back and prepared to push in again, but she pushed me off of her and ran from the bed to the bathroom.

I lie in the bed concerned and puzzled. I asked Leslie if she was alright when she returned from the bathroom, and she apologized and said she merely had to pee from being nervous. Her song of choice was rapidly fading, and she urged me to enter her again while it was still playing. As we pushed and pulled at each other a few more times, Leslie seemed to be getting into it. I was having trouble feeling much of anything through the condom, but the situation itself was enough to keep me hard. I felt like I might even be able to come, a feat quite difficult for me when sheathed in latex. Then Leslie pushed me off and ran to the bathroom again. This time she stayed there for a while. It was rather obvious that Leslie had more than a nervous bladder.

The night went on like that, with us poking for a minute

or two, and then Leslie bolting to the bathroom to let loose her bowels while I waited in the bed keeping myself alive. As it turns out, despite the fact that she was very beautiful, Leslie thought of herself as fat, and a friend at school had turned her on to the weight loss wonders of Ex-Lax.

We tried it again in a few days, and it went better, and then after having irregular sex for the next month, Leslie dumped me. She said, "It always seems to mean so much to you; I just want to get fucked." That was the first time I encountered the notion that nice girls might actually like dirty, filthy, hot sex, and I knew for certain that's what she had in mind to give to the next guy.

By the fall of 1998, when I was living in my parents' house again, I was long past my enchantment with virgins. I found them to be teases for the most part, and I had no interest in being the guy who had to ease them through the gauntlet of societal repressions.

Of course, living in my parents' laundry room meant that I was done with many things where women were concerned. I was also working in the electronics department of Target, and when one is clad in a red polo shirt and khaki pants, the odds of meeting women are reduced even further. Needless to say, I spent most of my spare time staring at the monochrome screen on my cheap laptop computer (which connected to America Online at a whopping 2600 bps), surfing the chat rooms and looking for someone to have phonesex with.

One girl that I spoke with on a regular basis, Marceil, was quite charming. Not only did she have the most filthy mouth and outrageous capacity for conjuring hot fantasies, she was exceptionally well read and interesting. We spent half our time masturbating together, and the other half discussing Thomas Hardy and Albert Camus.

We spoke for most of the year, then before I sojourned to back Central New York to complete graduate school, we decided to meet. I drove the six hours from Charlotte, North Carolina, to Opelika, Alabama. Not to disparage the good people of Opelika, but if they are under the delusion that theirs is a cosmopolitan town, then their view of civilization has not progressed much past the bronze age. Being from the south, you would think that I might feel at home anywhere that grits and venison are a staple food. But I am from the south of suburbs and gentility; I am a vegetarian, and that immediately alienates me from my backwoods brethren.

I dealt with the discomfort of my surroundings, and got a room at the newest motel in town, the Super 8. Eerily enough, as soon I was in my room the phone started ringing. It was Marceil, my delicious phonesex princess.

"How did you know I was here?" I asked.

"There's no place else you could be in this town," she said. Marceil did not drip with a lazy, southern accent as most of her townspeople did. (Even *I* had trouble understanding the drawled enunciation of the desk clerk while negotiating my room.) Marceil was a transplant from Pittsburgh—her mother had married a Methodist minister after leaving her husband for him, and thus when she told me that my choices of whereabouts were few and far between within the city limits, it was with a disdain that I could understand: the town I grew up in is also small, though we do not even share the luxury of a hotel.

I drove to pick up Marceil at the veterinary clinic where she worked as an assistant. I took this to mean she fed the animals and cleaned their cages, and this fact was confirmed when she entered my car. However, she was much prettier than her photos had indicated, and so I did not allow the odor of caged animals to put a damper on our rendezvous.

Back at the motel we each sat on a different bed and asked awkward questions of one another. The questions were awkward because they had no point; they were merely an attempt to mask the surreal aspect of meeting someone in person who has previously only been an abstract voice. It was true that Marceil had once implored me to come and visit, take her to an adult theater, and fuck her in the ass while dozens of anonymous men took turns sodomizing her mouth. But sitting on the bed opposite her, I found it impossible to reconcile the rather proper and innocent girl before me with the absolute whore that spoke to me on the phone.

After about an hour she mentioned that she would have to be getting home soon, and for some reason I chose that moment to begin my seduction of her. As are usually the case with these things, it was not the long, slow, ritualistic dance into the bliss of the bed, but rather brief, confusing, and clumsy.

As soon as my hands were down her pants and playing with her pussy, she suggested that we wait until tomorrow night, when we had more time. I agreed with her, but I had a raging erection, and I had driven for a considerable distance (which, sadly, was not the longest distance I have ever driven for sex.) After mutually deciding that we should put off our passions for just a few more hours, we were back on top of one another. We dove straight into intercourse with such speed that neither one of us had our pants completely off. I was so aroused that the condom didn't give me a lick of trouble, and no sooner was it on than it was off again as I came on Marceil's face and shirt. I would spend most of the drive to her place apologizing about the shirt.

When I went to pick her up the next day, my car wouldn't start. The rest of my weekend became an ordeal in finding a mechanic in Opelika who would fix my car without raising the price to an absurd amount because of my out-of-state plates. None of Marceil's friends would give her a lift to the motel, because they thought meeting a guy from the internet was the most insane thing a person could do. I freely admit that choosing a partner from the internet probably increases the likelihood of selecting certain undesirable traits (for example, the ability to sit inside in the dark and stare at a computer screen hypnotically for hours), but the ratio of psychos to "normal people" is no greater in the virtual world than it is elsewhere. And besides, the odds still say you're more likely to be killed in an auto accident. Or by a relative.

Without a car, and without willing friends to ferry her to me, Marceil and I were out of luck. I did not see her again for the remainder of my agonizing stay in her fair city, and when I returned to the darkness of my parents' laundry room, kneeled beside my bed with cock in hand and phone to head, Marceil dropped a bomb on me:

"I was a virgin, you know. I should have told you."

Because it seemed impossible to me that a virgin could have articulated such intense sexual desire, I thought that she said she was a *Virginian*, that she wasn't from Pittsburgh at all, but a southerner like me. And then I realized how stupid that was.

"Oh," I said. I thought about what my response should be. Why was she telling me this now? Was I supposed to feel special? Guilty? I actually did feel kind of lousy. I didn't feel as though I had given her an encounter to remember, and that if anything I may have just made her feel cheap and used. "So, like, why didn't you tell me?"

"I didn't care," she said. "It wasn't a big deal. Besides, I'm only--" And at hearing her actual age, I came from sheer fright. "I have a lot of years ahead of me to really make it matter." I heard the words, but my head was swimming from the crushing weight of incontrovertible truths, of the sort usually reserved for bodice-rippers and television mini-series.

Where did her attitude come from? Crossing that initial and thrilling sexual threshold has always seemed of monumental consequence, regardless of your age or culture or class. So much of the world that we experience is a reaction to the mystery of sexuality, a mystery that we can only begin to unravel with the aid of an accomplice. It was beyond my scope of reason to grasp how Marceil was undaunted by the union of bodies and constriction of muscles that weigh upon the minds of most people.

Even though I had felt her body against mine, she became more abstract to me in the light of her confession. Her yielding of her virginity without pomp and circumstance set her apart from my construction of what a woman was in my mind. I was threatened by it—she seemed to have a fearlessness that made her stronger than me. I was a fool the night I lost my virginity, and I was a fool many times after that: when I was with a woman I pretended to be someone I was not; I wore the mantle of manliness that I believed was proper, instead of allowing myself to open up to someone and free the well of desire that I had dammed inside of myself out of shame.

But it would be a while yet before I could find the ease with which to free myself, and so my phone calls to Marceil became more infrequent until she became an abstraction entirely: a memory, like everything else eventually becomes.

Touched

I found the ad in the back of *Rolling Stone*. It was a classified ad with small print promising that after one call you would be "cumming back for more." I called the number, which was international, and waited as the foreign tone rang a few times. When my call went through, a seductive, automated woman's voice welcomed me and tossed around sexual innuendo for a few minutes, then scolded minors who might have called and urged them to hang up. (I imagine that few adolescents were ever deterred.) I was then dumped immediately onto a party line, where what sounded like dozens of people, both men and women, were moaning with ecstasy. It would have been impossible to try and carry on a conversation over that din of desire, and so it seemed everyone had spontaneously erupted in a chorus of coming. The sound of other people's pleasure was still a rarity for me then; I was a junior in college, but the promises of frequent sorority servicing in college did not pan out for me as they did most of my friends—in retrospect, I see that the girls could sense I dripped with desperation, the same way a soldier still green from boot camp sweats with eagerness and anxiety to finally fire his weapon at a live target. Needless to say, I was avoided *exactly* like someone who was fast on the trigger. Thus, when I heard those cries of release on the phone, I came brutally and quickly myself. I felt terribly guilty for some reason afterward, but the guilt was not substantial enough to prevent me from calling back an hour later.

When the phone bill arrived a few weeks after my initial

call, I had managed to tally a modest one hundred and fifty dollars in phone calls. Had I been the sole resident of my domain, the bill would have presented little problem, but I lived in my parents' house during my junior and senior years of college. I was also unemployed. At the time, it really didn't register with me that I was an unemployed guy studying poetry while masturbating chronically in my parents' basement. The whole lack-of-getting-laid thing makes perfect sense now.

Naturally, my parents flipped out when they saw the chunk of change that my jerking off had cost them. I explained the matter as a misunderstanding on my part: I had recently learned how to connect via modem to other computers, and I had errantly dialed up a number to an academic site without realizing it was in another country. I apologized profusely and my dad assigned me extra yard work (which was actually worse than it might sound: we lived on several acres that required constant tending). I knew I only had one shot with that excuse, and so I would have to be resilient and avoid the temptation to dial-for-delight.

I went out that night, purchased a copy of *Hustler*, and nearly wrecked my car as I drove home at a speed that would have garnered felony charges, all the while scanning the picture-plentiful phone sex ads. It was such a thrill for me to listen to other people come that whenever I looked at a phone my dick began to swell. The next eight months, as the phone bills continued to escalate and I was forced to get a job, I concocted one sci-fi excuse after another: the higher the phone bill, the more inane my explanation for why I was calling small Caribbean islands. My dad had been a college professor, and even though he had spent the previous ten years working in the private sector, surely not even he could have believed that housed in the tropics was a wealth of mainframe computers that contained volumes of new critical work on the Metaphysical poets.

If my phone sex obsession had resulted in any actual human interaction, it might make more sense as to why I had to have it so badly. However, I never spoke a single word during any of the calls I made. I would whack myself to the point of drawing blood as I listened to horny, lonely voices talking or cooing to one another, and thus I became a voyeur of loneliness, which is probably the loneliest thing you can be.

A recurrent pattern in many of these calls was the indifferent operator. It was the job (in theory) of whatever girl was acting as operator to help cultivate sexual discussion on the line. On most occasions, her boredom with the constant barrage of men calling for a quick jerk session was heavily evident, and you could sometimes hear her flipping magazine pages, or the sound of her changing television channels.

My parents finally kicked me out of the house when one of the bills topped five hundred dollars. I moved in with my friend David, promptly started running up his phone bill, and then somehow persuaded him to cash in his trust fund and loan me the money to pay the bill. David's nest egg that had been accruing interest since his birth was depleted rapidly, and when the well was dry I departed for Central New York to attend graduate school. I left David with a four hundred dollar phone bill, which was a more unkind cut after learning a week prior to my departure that he and his girlfriend had become pregnant. Serious cocaine addicts have behaved in more a honorable fashion to the family members that they fuck over in order to support their habits, and my failings as a human being were simply a direct result of my inability to jerk off without some sort of pornographic stimuli.

I thought that when I arrived in New York I would finally get the monkey off my back, but my phone was shut off after only a week of service. I had racked up a long distance bill of such magnitude in such a short period of time that it alarmed the telephone company. My first three years in New York were spent with spotty phone service because I was always frightfully behind on my bill. It was, after all, higher than my rent by a long shot, and I was at least rational enough to realize I needed a place to live more than phone sex.

I emphasize again, however, that I was only *listening* during these calls as I held my breath and pounded myself vigorously in silence. Once I began to actually speak, things got worse, and my maxim of rent-before-phone-sex was left behind like the furniture I had to abandon in the numerous apartments I fled in order to avoid eviction.

I learned to speak my desire in the same place I had learned to listen: in my parents' basement, in the room directly under their bedroom. It was about six on Christmas morning, and I had met an older woman in a chat room on AOL who wanted to get off on the phone. I had butterflies in my stomach as I dialed her number, and I came shortly after we began to talk, even though we weren't doing much more at that point than just describing ourselves. For the remainder of my visit at my parents' over the holidays I was attendant to only one thing: the computer. I would hang out in a chat room on AOL (usually the "All Men Do It" room), and when a woman materialized in the room, I would join the swarm of other lurking masturbators who flooded her with instant messages that pleaded to be the one she chose to play with. When I returned to school, I promptly filled out the paperwork for a student loan so I could buy my own computer, and have a little extra cash to cover my phone bills.

The knowledge that there was a woman who was listening to me as I pleasured myself, and who was very likely doing the same thing, was the most delightful notion—sometimes even more wonderful than sex. Sound is the most pleasurable of the senses for me, and the orgasmic orchestra that I helped conduct over the phone was a constant source of arousing and heavenly music. The sound of any random woman coming is the sound of a beautiful woman—your ears are never as biased as your eyes. When I closed mine and listened to a woman evoke such primal sounds from the instrument of her body, I felt the strings of pleasure within my own body begin to vibrate, and my hand would keep tempo along my cock until the crescendo.

In my initial conversations with women I was very coy. We would talk for a while about non-sexual topics, then build through a slow foreplay until we were both moaning and diddling ourselves towards mania. However, like many addicts, the casual nature of my addiction spiraled all too quickly to a single point: to get my fix. Even when I had a girlfriend, all I wanted to do was get on the computer, find someone to talk to, and fall to my knees and jerk off while on the telephone. I had several people that I talked to on a regular basis, and when I knew they would be online I *had* to be in front of the computer to greet them and invite them to join me for a session of self-gratification. I left parties to go home and jerk off on the phone; I cut actual dates short. Even when I knew that my girlfriend was on her way over and that I would *definitely* be getting laid, I would have phone sex and completely ruin my appetite for real, live intimacy.

With the fat government loan checks rolling in every semester, my appetite for whacking via the assistance of Bell

Atlantic was insatiable. I eventually phoned beyond my means and lost phone service completely. I was able to dial out using prepaid calling cards, and I spent all my rent money for the next two months doing that. During that time I somehow became engaged to another graduate student in the English Department: during an argument that stemmed from her inability to reach me via the telephone I said, "Well, if we're going to care this much about each other, we might as well get married."

"Okay," she said, and a few days later she and I went to get a marriage license. I moved in with her shortly after that, but not because I wanted to join my life with hers in any sort of permanent sense: I had to vacate the apartment I was in because my landlords were threatening to evict me. I stole away under cover of night during the course of three days as I stealthily transported my meager belongings one carload at a time to my fiancée's, all the while realizing that I would have to contain my urges for telephone titillation once I shared the same space as my bride to be.

While I was able to restrain my need to reach out and touch someone (anyone, really), I still was jerking off like a man possessed. I would sneak out of the bed and go into the living room, which was carpeted, and kneel in front of the television and masturbate to the female meteorologists on *The Weather Channel.* One night my fiancée caught me taking the happy pup for a walk, and from that day forward made it her habit to walk barefoot across the entirety of the carpet to discover the evidence of my onanism. (For the laymen, allow me to point out that when semen is expelled onto carpet, it often leaves a crusty spot that one can feel if it isn't cleaned up immediately after landing.) She became suspicious of me when I would vacuum, as though I were constantly trying to cover up my tracks—*pecker tracks* as my mother used to call them.

Ultimately, I broke down and commenced with the phone play again, only to be caught fairly quickly by my dear would-be-life-long love. We didn't have call waiting, and after trying to call one day and finding the phone line busy, she called the phone company to check on the bill. Her assumption was that I was on the line having phone sex, and much to her credit, she was right. That night *she* packed my things and moved them into the corridor of our apartment building. I was at a Ratdog concert while this was happening, and when I arrived at home to find my things waiting for me silently in the hallway, I figured my dreams of holy matrimony weren't going to pan out.

I landed on the spare futon of my friend Hooper, and his roommate, T.J. I confess to being a slow learner, which is why once I realized I had a virgin phone line at my disposal I began my obsessive behavior all over again. Because I was broke, I couldn't go out and do anything, and because I was stuck at home, I had nothing to turn to but my own ambrosia, the telephone.

By the end of the summer the phone bill had escalated to approximately $4500. I eventually paid it, with the majority of my student loan for that semester, and T.J. took me to the bank (literally) to have a letter notarized stating that I was the sole culprit responsible for the slow payment on the long distance charges for adult entertainment lines. I felt that T.J. was out to humiliate me because I had often knelt outside his bedroom and masturbated as I listened to him fuck his girlfriend. Sometimes I was even on the phone as I did this.

Ultimately I did unhinge myself from the shackles of aural delights. I mean, there's only so much phone sex a person can take. But when I consider what attracted me to it, I suspect it was because I lacked the savvy and skill to be the lover in life that I was on the phone, and whatever desires I kept from my partner at the time seemed completely easy to reveal to the abstract voices that urged me to orgasm. The same was true for the women I spoke with as well: there was the woman from New York city, a nurse, who told me how she loved to suck her brother's cock, and on one occasion someone that she claimed was her brother *did* walk in on her having phone sex with me, and I shot a massive load as I listened to her gagging on his dick. There was an eighteen year-old in D.C. who was supposedly from an upper class family who begged me to call her a worthless whore while her dog licked her pussy. I heard couples having sex, vibrators in cunts, voices whispering urgently for me to fuck them as their husbands or parents or boyfriends or roommates were asleep in the next room. I've had innumerable women on the phone ask me to tell them that I love them as they hysterically work themselves into a lather. I have been a party to more confessions of shame and sin and desperation that I can even begin to speculate about. I must have heard thousands of orgasms (or the illusion of orgasms). Whether or not any of it was true is irrelevant: I was a witness to those dark, misshapen desires that nested inside all those people, and I heard them temporarily become weightless as their passions went aloft into the ether of wires and satellite signals, and this is happening all around us, at all times: those frequencies we cannot detect with our senses are passing through our bodies, carrying not only the currents of pop culture to our televisions and radios, but also the shriek of orgasm from one attuned ear to another.

Oedipus Wrecked

My parents *had* to think that I had gone to the movies with my brother. It was the only explanation that seemed reasonable when I reached the top of the stairs and froze as I saw their entwined legs dangling from the edge of the couch. I heard my father's determined grunting, and my mother sounded either very sick or horny beyond the point of intelligible communication.

My mother actually was quite sick. Even though it was the day after Christmas, it was not the holidays that were the occasion for my visit. I had been staying at my childhood home for the past month because my mother had cancer. She told me that it was her *dying wish* to have all "her babies"— meaning my brother and me—at home for one last Christmas.

This was easy to accomplish because my younger brother (at 26) had yet to leave home. Also, my mother's impending demise was a thing of great suspicion on the part of everyone. No one doubted that she would survive the cancer: the tumor in her breast had been caught so early that it seemed as though the doctors didn't take her disease that seriously. Her prognosis for recovery was something like ninety-eight percent.

However, there was one complication: my mother had a bad heart. (She had often extolled this fact for years in a metaphorical sense; it was ironic that her malady became a literal one.) Because of her weakened coronary state, the mastectomy posed the risk of sending her into cardiac arrest.

Which was a risk she ran all the time to a certain degree.

Too much stress, over-exertion, over-excitement—these things could kill my mother. After I realized that my father was, indeed, *fucking my mommy* on the sofa, I thought about her heart pumping wildly in her chest and how it could simply give out at any moment. My father knew that, too, and so I wondered what might possess him to give mom a stiff poke with all the stress she was afflicted with anyway. My father had acquired the need for Viagra years ago (a prescription I had abused, to much amusement, from time to time), and so any sex he undertook was more or less premeditated.

Any concern for my mother's health quickly dissipated when I came to my senses and realized I was listening to my parents have sex. I turned to descend the stairs and immediately stepped on the one creaky spot in the steps that I first learned to avoid in high school when I would sneak out of the house. Clearly it had been awhile since I had needed to be covert about my comings and goings.

I did not move, but heard my mother say, "Howard..."

My dad didn't respond, keeping up his impassioned pace.

From where I was standing, we were out of sight of each other. I stayed put, loathing myself for invading the privacy of my parents in the midst of their intimacy. The shame I felt wasn't so much a result of the fact that I was hearing *my parents* have sex, but because I knew if the tables were turned—if I was on the couch with my girlfriend—my mother would be standing right where I was now, and she wouldn't feel the least built guilty for listening.

* * *

When I was sixteen my mother poisoned her boss. She didn't kill her, or even come close, but she did make her violently ill in a way that most people have probably dreamed of doing to one supervisor or another. I found this out when my mother came home from work that day, glowing in a manner that was uncharacteristic for her. I listened to her tale with marginal interest—I was still too naïve to imagine that my mother's madness could be turned against anyone that she loved as dearly as her family. She was, after all, still my mother, and not some fantastic version of a psychopathic, *Lifetime Channel*, movie-of-the-week mom, out to destroy the lives of everyone who crossed her in some capacity.

It was only three years later, while home on summer break after my first year of college, that I woke up with a knife to my throat and my mother screaming, "Get up you fucking bitch or I'll kill you! You don't sleep late in my goddamned house!" On the contrary, I had been sleeping late in her house for years. However, I was able to rouse myself out of bed quite quickly that morning. A few hours later, when I confronted my mom about her outburst, she had no idea what I was talking about. She would go on to have several episodes similar to this, but I wasn't around for most of them. I was able to escape to the safety and calm of college, a luxury that I felt my father and brother always held against me.

But no matter how far away I went, I could never escape her grasp. When I lived in central New York, as a graduate student, I ultimately had to disconnect my phone in order to abate her constant calling. And then she started calling the head of the English Department and leaving messages for *her baby*. It was usually her custom to be crying when she left these messages; when her guilt-tactics did not work on me directly, she was brilliant at enlisting the unwitting help of friends and colleagues who couldn't understand how I could be so cruel to a woman who obviously loved me so much.

Which was precisely the problem: her love for me was excessive. It was as if it was too much for her when I was four and suffering from pneumonia, and she stayed up for three nights straight with me in the hospital, looking at me on the other side of the oxygen tent where my lungs labored for air. Once I was freed from the tent, it was her protectiveness that began to shield me from the world, and then somewhere her love went astray.

Tell me, knowledgeable reader, if your mother doted upon your genitalia with pride, would this be a sign of her maternal love? My mother has grabbed my crotch so many times since I was sixteen and made a lewd comment about my size that I've lost count. She does this to my brother as well (though, curiously, I've never seen her do this to my father), and despite our protests it has continued.

How does one reconcile this behavior with the fact that I have always counted on my mother to take care of me when no one else would? And she has. And I have always found this to be one of her most noble qualities.

When I was 21, I inadvertently killed my father's wiener dog, Max. (Have there been acts committed that were more unbelievably Freudian? Even my therapist suggested that I was lying because it was, "simply too perfect" to be true.) I was driving a rather large van at the time, and the wiener dog was known to roam freely about our property. When I pulled into the driveway, the dog ran in front of me, and I stopped. He crossed in front of the car safely, I drove forward, and as I did so he ran back under one of the van's rear tires. It broke his back, and he died gasping for breath as I cradled him. When Max had expired I ran to my mother, weeping, begging for forgiveness, not entirely ignorant of the fact that

I carried my father's limp wiener (dog) to my mother, asking
for her love.

My father came home from work early, walked into my
room, and tore every book from the shelf. From where I
stood outside, I believe I heard him refer to me as a bastard
more than five times. Max was buried at a private service, to
which I was not invited, and an 8x10 glossy photo of him sits
on an end table in the living room, just a few inches from
where my parents' sweaty heads are pressed together right
now. Whenever anyone from outside the family inquires
about the photo to my parents, they respond with, "That's
Max, the dog our oldest son murdered."

But when I was living back at home in the fall of 1998
while on a break from graduate school, she had *my* dog sent
to the pound without my knowledge. She carried out the
deed as I slept (indeed, as I *slept late in her house*). I had
stayed up all night chatting on the net and jerking off, and so
if there was a struggle (which I doubt there was, because that
was the sweetest dog you've ever met), I was oblivious to it.
When I questioned my mother about my dog, she claimed
she knew nothing of it. She did, however, give me a lecture
about how irresponsible I was to let my dog run free without
proper oversight. She concluded the lecture by telling me it
was my own fault if my dog was gone.

Some years later, my mother claimed that an angel of the
Lord visited her, and she admitted to having the Animal
Control Department cart my dog to the death chamber. I
can't say I was particularly surprised. As a point of fact, she
had made at least two other pets of mine disappear in a
similar manner during the course of my upbringing.

Around the time she confessed to being the culprit in the
case of my disappearing dog, she confessed to many other
things. (The angel that visited her had apparently "washed

her soul clean," so that my mother felt she could admit to past transgressions since they had all been forgiven by the Lord. The morning after her vision, she flushed all of her prescription medications down the toilet—and from the quantities of antidepressants and sleeping pills and pain relievers that I know she kept, I'm sure that was more than a single flush. I have not yet decided if her sudden distaste for her little helpers was a result of her "healing," or a desire to never encounter an angel of the Lord again.) Among the many other things that she confessed was that she never poisoned her boss, and that she remembered all too well the morning she held a knife to my throat while I overslept that one summer.

This was a complete mindfuck to me. Why tell your sixteen year-old son that you poisoned your boss? I'm not sure if it's more insane to confide a secret like that if it's true, or to make it up for shits and giggles and pass it off as the truth. It doesn't matter. Not long after my mother cavalierly told me that yarn, I became obsessed with people potentially putting things in my beverage, and for years I would insist that drinks be brought to me in bottles with the cap still intact.

And holding a knife to my throat? And lying about it all these years, and not just to me, but to my dad and brother, both of whom were sufficiently convinced by her account to dismiss my own recollection as a vivid dream?

When I was around ten, and not long after I had my first erection spring up on a warm summer day as I lay nude in the sun with my mother (upon my dong's rising, my mother proudly led me inside to display my engorged member to my father), I began playing a new "wrestling" game with the girl next door. She was a few years younger than me, but she seemed just as delighted as I to roll around in the grass and feel me "pin her" as my hard, young cock nuzzled her white skin through my corduroys. One day I looked up to see my mother smiling at me through the kitchen window, and later she said, "I saw what you were doing today. I know you weren't wrestling."

Her tone was not at all disapproving, as most parents might react. It was more conspiratorial, as if she wanted me to confide in her about my confusing urges, make her a participant somehow.

When I was older, she passed by me one night as I went to the bathroom, and her hand lashed out for my crotch. I turned quickly, and she instead grabbed my pocket, feeling something hard inside.

"What do you have there? Is that my Vaseline? Are you going to whacky-whacky?" She punctuated this with the universal hand gesture for male masturbation, and stuck her tongue out to one side of her mouth.

I most likely told her to shut-up, or something to that effect, because she suddenly began to treat me as though as I had been caught stealing money from her.

"Show me what you have in your pocket. Give it to me now. You're not jerking off with my Vaseline. Give it." I pleaded with her not to humiliate me, and after she had extracted enough remorse from me, she moved on. I went into the bathroom, and removed her vibrator from my pocket; her Vaseline was already in there.

I angrily shoved the vibrator up my ass as I jerked off, hating my mother for nearly discovering my secret pleasure. I didn't understand the way she behaved, wanting to shame me, because she had told me that she had felt shame often as a child, at the hands of her tormentors, her siblings.

There was the time her younger brother and his friends nearly raped her. There was the other time when her older sisters and their boyfriends ran her down and stripped her and made fun of her for being on the rag. And being from a poor, farming family from the Appalachian Mountains, her tampon was quite literally a rag. She made a point about this, and about the other conditions of her poverty: having to share a bed, outdoor plumbing, cracks in the floor so wide you could see the chickens that lived under the house. She goes to great lengths to underscore to my bother and I just *how poor she was*. Most often these stories come up when we have gone for a suitable amount of time without giving her another reason to inflict guilt on us.

I didn't really think about that too much as I knelt in the bathroom, plundering myself with my mother's vibrator. I listened for the sound of her footsteps approaching the door, to burst in on me, or eavesdrop on my ministrations, all the while simply trying to come.

And how can I say to you, kind reader, that when I stood on those steps listening to my parents' lovemaking, the ultimate sound I listened for was not the finale of orgasm, but the end of my mother's life? I thought of her heart heaving in her heavy chest, the smallness of the tumor that harbored the weight of a star that had collapsed on itself, my father's meaty body balanced on hers like a bulldozer—I wanted him to fuck her to death. I saw no more fitting end to my mother's life than to die by the dick, the very dick she claimed never to have put in her mouth in thirty years of marriage, and I wanted her to die because no child should ever need to know that sort of information about his parents.

But I also wanted to make some sort of move, some noise to alert them to my presence so that they might stop. I did not want my mother to die in that instant, even though her life was a ceiling to my own, and I longed for nothing more than to be free of her canopy of misguided intentions. I started up the steps again.

In my moment of princely indecision they had concluded their activities, and my father was collapsed in my mother's arms, his head on her breasts that would be gone at the end of the week. He looked like Odysseus, unlashed from the mast and clinging to the rocks, called by the song of the siren's heart.

from *Are You There God? It's Me. Kevin.* (2008)*

*I did not come up with that title, and I absolutely hate it; I want that fact noted for all time.

Interlude with the Vampire
(*AYTG?IM.K.* Mix)

[Allow me for a moment to return to the subject of truth that I touched upon in the preface to this collection. The observant reader will notice that there are two versions of the story "Interlude with the Vampire" contained herein. Both are entirely true; neither is entirely true *as it is told*. I can practically hear some of you crying out, "Dirty pool!" Well, not entirely. I expect that the people reading my work—the obsessive readers, the loiterers of literature—might be wise to the fact that I like to play little games. Such is the case in one of the versions of these stories: I make it very plain which story is to be least trusted, and I do it by summoning our old friend Nathaniel Hawthorne to the party. I pose the same choice to you as he did in "Young Goodman Brown," another fellow who shared my curiosity for being out well past the hour when all decent folk have gone to bed.]

With the exception of a few nights when I had far too much to drink, I can't recall doing any genuine praying until my grandfather's death. (There were occasions of feigned reverence, of course, but nothing authentic.) And even after the funeral it was because the Sundays accumulated so quickly in those following weeks that going to church was an easy habit to pick up again, the ritual of the black suit, the bowed head, the strained stoicism of the bereaved.

At first the prayers were the mumbled memories I'd not recited in a long while: the Apostle's Creed, the Lord's Prayer... and I spent the quiet moments of personal reflection wondering just what the fuck I was doing seated amongst people whom I considered to be only a glass of Kool-Aid away from total insanity.

More often than not I was spending prayer time thinking about the previous evening's bout with Lorraine, who spent her Sunday mornings and afternoons sleeping off her hangover in my bedroom, letting the room simmer with that unique brand of human odor that is only produced by the bodies of alcoholics ridding themselves of the night's poisons.

But a man can only take being slapped around by a pretty girl with fantastic tits for so long. I imagine that a lot of men would ultimately cross that threshold where they resort to their primal instincts and let loose the beast—I wanted that to happen to me, and I had visions of antiquated masculinity overtaking me in the same fashion as the Hulk bursting forth from the small frame of Bruce Banner. However, no burst of rage ever manifested at the crucial moment, and I can only assume that my lack of aggression is a sign of my advanced evolution, like the fact that I was born with only three wisdom teeth. Or it is a sign that I am a giant pussy.

Either way, I'd been humbled enough by Lorraine that it wasn't such a large leap to humble myself a little further and express my troubles to the indifferent cosmos:

Holy Nada, in Whom I do not believe, throw me a bone here. If you exist, if you are listening, if you aren't too fucking busy ignoring the suffering of the children of Africa, could you send me a good woman? Because I've been trying. I've been giving it my best shot, and I feel like I need a little bonus here, like a hot set of twins or something. Also, if you pay attention to this prayer and none at all the ones about stopping war, you've really got to get your priorities in order... And one more thing: I know you've probably been hearing this a lot lately after the Redsox sweeping the series, but what about the Cubs?

I stared at the mute cross that floated above the pulpit; it was suspended by thin wires to create a mystical illusion, and I found myself wishing those wires would snap and impale the minister. And not because I had any disdain for the minister—he was genuinely one of the truest Christians I've ever met. It's just that I was in the mood for an Old Testament God, the proactive one with a taste for arson and a gambler's sensibility. The one who knew how to send a message. This New Testament God, with his (or her—I don't know or care) warm fuzzies approach—all puppy dogs and ice cream—really sucked. "Turn the other cheek," Jesus advised. I was getting beat up by my woman; I turned my cheeks all too regularly. Where were my locusts, my plague of retribution?

At the end of the service, before I'd even had time to rise from the pew, a woman's voice said:

"Kevin?"

I turned around; an attractive brunette in her late 30s was staring at me. I began to mentally recant all the blasphemous statements I'd ever made in my life. These were incredibly fast results. Apparently praying was like dealing with Ticketmaster: sometimes you buy tickets the day of the show and for unexplainable reasons you end up in the front row.

"Hi," I said. I didn't know what else to say. I assumed she knew the reason why she was talking to me, and she did:

"Do you think you'd be interested in teaching our high school Sunday school class? We're having a tough time finding someone who will stick with it, and your name was suggested to me."

I looked down in my lap at the church bulletin and began

to fold and refold it into a tiny square of waste. My honest thought at the moment was, *Well, if I don't do it they'll probably end up with some right-wing wacko who teaches them to hate fags and abortionists.* I was so baffled by the request to have me lead a Sunday school class that I wasn't struck by the curiosity of the timing until after I'd agreed to do it and was firing up a joint on the drive back home.

The following Sunday I woke up two hours before I had to be at the church. I took a bong hit—several, actually—and considered what I was going to tell a group of high school kids about Christianity. If someone stopped me on the street and asked for a lesson in Christian doctrine I'd say: "It's fairly fucked up. But try to be nice to everyone. That's about all you need to know." I doubted that would go over well at the church.

I tried to recall my own Sunday school classes from when I was younger, but all I could think of was a craft activity in which one used yarn, glitter, and construction paper to make the animals of Noah's Ark. And even though all of those items could be found in my apartment (I'd rather skip the explanation for why this was the case) there was no way I was leading a craft activity. I was at least sharp enough to know that teenagers would greet such a task with a disdain usually reserved for war criminals. Or parents. The lunacy of the whole situation very quickly had me hyperventilating and I went to my pill stash for a Valium. Then I made myself a mimosa and tried to relax until it was time to leave.

The high school kids had their Sunday school class in what was known as the "Youth Room." It was the church's way of establishing a fun and safe environment for the children. It earned its name because the room had couches and a Foosball table. Clearly, comfortable seating and table soccer is the line of demarcation between adolescence and adulthood. Perhaps not so strangely, I felt right at home.

When I arrived at the classroom I found four people waiting on me. They were all sitting on a single sofa. I mumbled a greeting and took a seat on the couch opposite theirs. I stared at the faces in front of me. A father and his three children. It was obvious that someone had made them come to the class so I'd have someone to talk to. The father, a deacon in our church, was clearly present for reconnaissance purposes. The children appeared to be there because they'd been threatened with parental retaliation.

I made an attempt to use all my stalling tactics that I'd learned to put to good use in the literature courses I taught at the local community college. I asked everyone's name and where they were from. In a college class this works out well because I'm dealing with a diverse group of individuals. With four people who are related it's an icebreaker that sinks as quickly as you might guess.

I picked up a Bible that was laying beside me on the couch.

"Is anyone familiar with Ecclesiastes?"

The quartet shook their heads side to side solemnly and in unison. This is the primary problem with religious folk: very few of them bother to read the text that they allegedly follow. Personally, whenever I'm dealing with matters involving my soul for all eternity, I like to read the fine print.

"Well," I said as I flipped to the proper page, "let's talk about vanity," and I proceeded to monologue for thirty minutes on the pointlessness of life. The basic premise of Ecclesiastes might be summed up this way: you're going to die, there's nothing you can do about it, you will never understand the world and what it means, thus you should just sit back, relax, get a good woman and love her as hard as

you can. *Vanity of vanities! All is vanity!* That was how the
book began. It was an idea that was heavy on my mind. Over
the preceding few weeks, after my grandfather's death, I'd
watched the sum of a man's life reduced to a few boxes of
photographs and mementos. Everything else was
transformed into trash as easily as taking a breath, and that
last breath scattered memory to dust.

My hometown was being demolished as well. The rolling
hills and fields that bordered the lake had become
constellations of Charlotte, and bankers by the thousands
orbited the city from the safety of their identical condos and
houses. They left a comet trail of Wal-Marts, Ruby Tuesday's,
Applebees, and flimsy strip malls in their wake. No matter
how well the attempt is made, a Wal-Mart constructed of
faux marble in a neo-classical mode is still a garish sight.

When I concluded my talk about Ecclesiastes the kids
were all staring at their shoes. The father slapped his hands
on his knees, stood, shook my hand and said, "Good stuff.
Uplifting." He didn't seem the type of person inclined to
nuanced sarcasm, so I accepted that he was sincere. His kids
followed him out of the room without a word to me. I spent
the worship service in the Youth Room practicing Foosball
on the church's criminally underused table.

The following Sunday I expected—perhaps even prayed—
to find an empty room welcoming me. Alas, the same three
siblings were there, but they'd brought a few friends. A tiny
portion of me wanted to explain to them how uncool it is to
invite people to church—but I was thirty-one years old.
Maybe church had become hip and I was unaware. I doubted
it, but I wasn't willing to risk the ridicule of a group of
teenagers. I remember that cruel adolescent angst quite well,
and I had no desire to be its target again. This time, though,

there was no deacon overseeing me, and so I settled back into a couch and talked for forty-five minutes about the problems of freewill in a universe controlled by physical laws. When I was done, a sixteen-year-old girl named Wendy said:

"So, like, what does this have to do with Jesus?"

I didn't have an immediate answer. As I was a little baked, and therefore a little snackish, I'd started thinking about the possibility of a grilled cheese in my future.

"Well, you know Wendy... Okay. Here it is: Because you're made of the same basic molecules as everything else in the Universe, you're subject to the laws of physics, and yet it seems as though we're immune from that because we make choices. Or seem to. So are we making choices, or are our choices really just the result of forces in the Universe acting upon us?"

"Well, duh," she said, leaning forward and shaking her head at me. "Of course some force is acting on us. We call that the Holy Spirit."

I looked around the room. The other kids were nodding in agreement. I picked up a Bible and threw it at Wendy's head. She was quicker than she looked and batted it down before it made contact.

"What are you doing? Are you freaking crazy?"

"No, I just want to ask you a question: did I decide to throw that Bible or did the Holy Spirit make me do it?"

Over the next few weeks more kids would trickle in each Sunday until the couches were filled to capacity. I couldn't figure it out. What we discussed in the Youth Room was so antithetical to typical Christian belief that I expected the Inquisition to visit me at any moment with charges of heresy—evolution, abortion, teen sex, drugs. This was not the

stuff that most parents would be happy about their children
hearing at school, let alone church. And my stances on the
issues were what you might expect:

Evolution: "You can believe in God and evolution. Darwin
did."

Abortion: "It's not a form of birth control, kids. But would
you rather use a doctor or a coat hanger?"

Drugs: "All the movies made about marijuana are
comedies. Movies about cocaine and heroin are tragedies. If
you need it spelled out more definitively than that I
recommend you stay away from drugs."

But the Inquisition never came knocking. In fact, parents
stopped me in the corridors and parking lot of the church to
tell me what good things they'd heard from their children. I
wanted to say, "You realize I'm only a pussy hair away from
total inebriation, right? You know I've swallowed more pain
pills just this morning than most people would consider
advisable in a day?" But my reply was always an embarrassed
'Thanks' and then I would walk as quickly as I could in the
most convenient direction.

I hated for those Sunday mornings to give way to the
afternoon. Lorraine would be waiting for me at the
apartment when I got home, ready to apologize for the night
before or pick up the pieces of the argument again. That is, if
she was awake. And if she wasn't awake I would have a few
hours of tense solitude, waiting to see what mood she would
be wearing when she emerged from the bedroom.

Because of this, those weekly occasions with the kids
became such sweet relief. Of course, the satisfaction was only
half-hearted. I read in their faces the trust of innocence, and
in their parents' faces the optimism of faith; I'd not seen
these things in the mirror for a long time. Quite simply, I did
not believe as they did, and it seemed rather deceitful to sit

amongst them and feign belief. My guilt about this weighed on me like a sack of silver, and yet I couldn't stop. It felt too good.

However, the one thing I never did was bring prayer into the Sunday school class. As I didn't believe in a personal God who was actually listening, I felt leading others in a prayer that appealed to this sensibility would be a cruel mockery. No one said anything about the absence of this universal ritual for several weeks until Polly, a tiny girl who seemed perpetually accident prone, meekly raised her hand:

"Why don't we ever pray in here?"

I'd been expecting this. "Well, I figure you have enough prayer time at the worship service."

She considered this. Kip, one of the siblings who'd been coming from the beginning, asked, "Do you think you can pray too much?"

"I think there's a point at which it gets repetitive. But it's probably one of the few things you can do to excess without hurting yourself." No one seemed to know what I was talking about, but I chuckled to myself anyway. Polly raised her hand again, and her sleeve dipped down to reveal a purple crescent.

"Why doesn't God answer prayers?"

"I don't have an answer for that. What do you mean?"

"I mean I keep praying and nothing happens. It's like..." She stopped. Her lower lip trembled.

I coughed into my fist. "Well."

"It's like no one is listening," she said, and I saw the tears beginning. I wasn't capable of coping. This was only a volunteer position.

"Everyone," I said, "let's help Polly out. Let's pray that Polly's prayer gets answered, and maybe if you have some of your own stuff you want addressed, throw that in there too."

I immediately closed my eyes and dropped my head; I was not open to further discussion.

Look fucker, I thought, *as for myself, I don't feel it's necessary to repeat things to an allegedly omniscient being. Besides, I'm not counting on you, but this girl is. So even though I have doubts about your listening skills, show me what an idiot I am.*

After what seemed like an appropriate amount of time I raised my head and said, "Okay then. Let's see if that gets results."

* * *

All of this mess was circulating in my mind as I was sitting in the sun in that brief interval before my next class. I felt utterly detached from myself—I was teaching literature at a mediocre community college to students who were forced to take the course as part of their graduation requirements. Books are really the only constant source of meaning in my life, and it was the very definition of despair on those tedious days when I had to lecture about *Walden* and found myself facing twenty-five completely indifferent students who were enrolled in the automotive technology program, dreaming of a future changing tires with Mercurial speed during a NASCAR race. Furthermore, I was teaching Sunday school. That alone was enough to disorient me, and if that wasn't enough Lorraine was always available to slap me silly.

I looked up as one of my students was sitting down beside me.

"So, you ever had any Absinthe before?"

The comment wasn't completely random; Daryl was a student in my American Literature class, and during a

lecture on Hemingway I was prompted to explain a reference
to Absinthe in a short story. He'd been the only other person
in the room besides me who was familiar with it.

I told him a friend had brought some back from Europe
several years before, when it was still illegal in the States,
and I'd tried it then.

"Did it fuck you up?" His tone lacked the voyeurism of
indulgence one might expect; it had a palpable clinical
nature to it.

"I didn't have enough."

"Well, if you ever want some, let me know; I keep it
around."

"You like it that much?"

"No, it's..." Daryl took a drag from his cigarette and
glanced around; we were more or less alone. "I practice
vampirism. It's part of a ritual."

I turned my head toward Daryl: he was a stocky country
boy with coal-black hair and muscles shaped by labor and
not the ridiculous repetition of weights; he looked directly
into my eyes, and his eyes were the color of slate. I'd gotten
used to students telling me completely bizarre and personal
things—people are always looking for an authority figure to
heap their issues on for some shred of absolution. And even
though this was quite possibly in the top three weirdo
admissions of all time, I thought it best not to laugh at his
confession. But it was hard to ignore the fact that I was
sitting in direct sunlight with a guy who claimed to be a
vampire. When I didn't say anything he said:

"How old do I look to you?"

"I don't know," I said. "Twenty-five?"

"I'm thirty-eight."

"You're older than I am."

"Get yourself a woman who treats you right. You'll feel

the difference in your blood." He smiled, exposing a
mouthful of beautiful white teeth, but he wasn't smiling at
me: an elderly woman shuffling along with her arms full of
library books had come up beside us.

"Daryl," she said, "we missed you in church last week."
Daryl stood up, "I missed y'all too, Miss Emmie. I was out
of town. Let me take those books for you." He took the books
from her and they began to walk in the direction of the
library. I overheard her say:

"The grass needs mowing at the house. Think you might
could get by this week? Arnold's just getting too old, and
with this Indian Summer..."

Before they were out of earshot Daryl turned back to me:

"Think about what I said. If you want to meet a nice girl I
know the place." I wasn't sure what a church-going, grass-
mowing vampire might have in mind when he said "nice
girl," but as tempting as the offer was (considering my own
circumstances at the time), I was fairly sure I didn't want to
find out.

When I got home that night I made the puzzling
discovery that my apartment was littered with confetti. Upon
closer examination I realized the confetti was actually the
pages of my journals, which Lorraine had taken great care to
manufacture into fantastically small pieces. I found a note in
the bathroom that read: *Fuck you, faggot.* I also found my
toothbrush in the toilet.

Lorraine wanted to get married; I didn't, and this was the
root of all our problems. I loved her—or thought that I did.
In retrospect I realize her beauty charmed me, because I did
not think of myself as beautiful. The one time we tried to
have a civil discussion about our future together she ended
up chasing me around the apartment with a BB gun. After
that I dealt with issues via my journal, and Lorraine had

clearly not liked what she had shamelessly read, which is essentially what I have just said: I wanted out. I could feel my heart beating in my throat, and I felt a wave of total despair. I could get another television, I could replace picture frames, but I could not undo this. I went into my room and pounded my fist on my bed. I was trying to be what I thought a good guy should be—patient, kind, all that fucked up Corinthians crap—but I really felt like nothing more than a total pansy.

Lorraine stayed at her parents that night, and the next day after class I asked Daryl just what he meant by a "nice girl."

"Come and see for yourself. I'm going there tonight."

"Where?"

"Purgatory."

I considered this. "On a Tuesday?"

I met Daryl at Jackalope's—a bar down the street from my apartment that catered to a clientele who enjoyed trying to watch twenty-seven athletic events at once on televisions of various dimensions. It was not my kind of bar, but they had my kind of waitresses, and I so I often went there and pined through pints, flirting anemically—my lack of competitive drive has permeated even my romantic sensibilities, and while I enjoy a modest amount of pursuit I quickly lose momentum if matters don't fall easily into my lap. I've found waitresses to be a particularly difficult dating demographic for me, much like strippers: part of their job is to give you a sense of possibility, and it takes a real pro to read the proper signs. I am by no means a pro.

And besides, after leaving the bar my nightcap consisted of returning home to a drunk girlfriend whose demeanor was a crapshoot: drunk and horny, drunk and angry, drunk and passed out—what were my choices if I did get lucky, with a waitress or a patron? There was no going back to my place, and if I lingered too long elsewhere, I would surely be missed at the place where I was supposed to be.

But I'd reached my breaking point. The death of my grandfather had the effect that death often has on people close to the deceased: it made me want to take advantage of my own time. Lorraine had been a bust for a long while, and it was stupid to think our relationship was going to get better. I'd been rationalizing things for a nearly a year, in much the same manner as all those battered women who make excuses for their violent partner.

Of course, I wasn't dealing with any of this in a healthy manner, but was instead sneaking out of my apartment (I told Lorraine I was going to spend the evening helping my dad sort through my grandfather's clothes and would be home late, to which she replied, "I don't fucking care, douche bag."), conspiring to meet some type of willing vampyress (I assumed), and then slink back into my apartment hoping not to get my ass kicked. Oddly, the whole scenario seemed very normal to me at the time.

When Daryl arrived he didn't even order a beer. I couldn't blame him; he was terribly out of place in Jackalope's—he looked as though he was on his way to an upscale meeting of *Dungeons and Dragons* enthusiasts: leather pants and a leather jacket on top of what could only be described as a pirate shirt. He looked out the window facing the street as he waited for me to finish my drink, and when we stood to leave he looked at me and said, "I like your shoes."

"Look," I said, once we were in the car. "Where are we going exactly?"

"Purgatory. It's a monthly gathering of the leather and

S&M community. And other people."

"People like vampires?"

"Yep."

"Don't take this the wrong way, but the vampirism... this is a metaphor, right? Like all those girls at Phish shows who dress up like fairies and go around spreading pixie...." I trailed off. I'd been watching Daryl as I spoke, and his bright incisors had disappeared behind a grimace.

"It's not a metaphor." He paused while Judas Priest serenaded the gap in conversation. After a few moments he smiled again. "Look, I know you. You're cool. Do yourself a favor and leave that fairy shit out of your conversations where we're going."

"Fair enough." I leaned back in my seat. "So what's with the absinthe?"

"Oh, that. Well, you know it's potent shit. Most people it just fucks up. But it won't even intoxicate a vampire. It's a test, you know. To see if you've got the gene."

"What gene?"

"The vampire gene."

A scientific debate with someone claiming the existence of a vampire gene seemed rather pointless. I let the matter slide.

"So, do you like, you know, bite necks?"

Daryl slowed for a yellow light, and when the car was stopped he turned to me and said:

"Do I look like I have fucking fangs to you?" He flashed his teeth.

"Uh, no."

"Yeah," and his face dropped. "It sucks. I just can't afford to have the work done. You'll meet people tonight who've got them. Some are quality dental work. Some just look like crap because people file their teeth—that's just insane. Some people get lucky by birth... But if I could afford them, I'd have them. In the meantime, these work." He reached in his jacket and tossed a small item wrapped in wax paper in my lap; I picked it up. It was a disposable scalpel.

"Oh," I said. I offered a weak chuckle, but I wasn't sure why.

My stomach began to churn. I handed the scalpel back to him as we were pulling into the parking lot of the club where Purgatory was happening. When we were out of the car he put his arm around my shoulder and said, "Tonight you'll feel like a new man." The leather of his jacket creaked in my ear. "I really love your shoes," he said again as we approached the door. "I've been looking for a pair just like that."

In my daily existence, I am most often dressed like a nine year-old on his way to baseball practice: Converse sneakers, jeans, and a jersey style t-shirt with the ¾ length sleeves. On more formal occasions I might switch out the jeans for khakis. On chilly nights, or on what I perceive to be ultra-formal occasions, I'll add a dress shirt (typically a blue oxford) to my ensemble, but as I never button the shirt it functions more as a dinner jacket. As I perceived "Purgatory" to be an ultra-formal event, I was dressed appropriately—I'd even gone so far as to add black socks and a matching belt, and it was that leather belt which was most similar to the wardrobes of the other attendees. I was surrounded by extras from *Interview with the Vampire*—or a Renaissance Festival. Either way, I felt very much like the Southern preppy in Count Dracula's court. As I surveyed the room I thought, *One or more of these people is very likely carrying a set of twelve-sided dice.*

My mood might have tepidly approached something close to genuine fear had we been in a place more "dungeon-esque." However, we were at bar known for its regular booking of tribute bands, such as Appetite for Destruction (Guns n' Roses), Zoso (Led Zeppelin), Nothin' But a Good Time (Poison), and SkaCago (a curiously popular Chicago cover band who played everything in a Ska style). A person clad in leather with honest-to-God fangs doesn't look at all threatening standing in front of a sign advertising 2-for-1 Jell-O shooters and $1.50 margaritas on Fridays.

After we'd paid our $10 cover (it seemed only fitting one should pay a nominal fee to gain entrance to Purgatory), I followed Daryl to the bar and ordered the best beer available—a Corona for Christ's sake! Oh, Purgatory indeed! I discreetly popped two Percocets in my mouth, crunched them up, and washed them down with that most mediocre of Mexican concoctions. I would have rather gone outside and smoked a bowl, but Daryl didn't exude the pleasant indifference of a weed aficionado. Besides, at the bar, he'd ordered a Red Bull. The one time I ordered a Red Bull I was up until five a.m. crapping a substance that I thought was certainly a harbinger of hospitalization. That alone was proof enough for me that people who drink that stuff are wired way differently than I am.

Daryl stood at such a distance from me that it was uncertain as to whether we actually knew each other or not. I've no doubt it was my khakis that were the source of his discomfort. I sat on a barstool and waited for the warm bliss of the Percs to wash over me, and watched as the medievally clad crowd circulated and exchanged greetings. Nine Inch Nails played over the PA at a conversation-friendly volume, and two people who seemed more on the druid side of things arranged a chair and a coffee table on the stage.

Whenever anyone saw Daryl they gave a slight bow or curtsy, according to their gender. His reply was a terse nod in every case. Whenever their eyes fell on me they all appeared to snarl. I smiled politely and raised my Corona.

This went on for some time, and as no one was speaking to me—including Daryl—I was soon tipping back my third Corona and considering a cab ride home. Nine Inch Nails had given way to something resembling the sounds of a genocidal massacre mixed with asphalt production, and it was decidedly not conversation friendly. The scene seemed a terrible waste of a buzz, and I felt as though I were literally buzzing. Humming, in fact.

A petite girl with purple streaks in her hair and ample piercings walked over to Daryl and curtsied. He smiled at her and opened his arms; when he embraced her he pressed his face into her neck. In addition to her thin black dress and dog collar, she was wearing a pair of bright white Keds that glowed under the black-lights. Daryl yelled at the girl:

"This is my friend, Kevin." The veins in his neck stood out, but he was still barely audible over the music. I leaned my head close to theirs.

"Heaven?" She said.

"Kevin," Daryl repeated.

"Oh." She turned to me and smiled and curtsied again.

Daryl pressed his lips to my ear. "Ok, you're all set. I've got stage business. I'll see you later. Or maybe not." He gave me what I can only characterize as a wicked smile. I grabbed his arm before he could walk away.

"What? What? Where are you going?"

"I'm going to the stage. Amanda is yours for the night. I set it all up. She'll treat you right."

"How do you know her?"

He smiled at me again: "She's a good source of food." I let go of his arm and he pressed into the crowd. As soon as he was gone Amanda leaned into me.

"I like your shoes," she said.

"Oh, yeah. Thanks. I like yours too. They glow."

She looked down in wide-eyed amazement: "Oh, they do, don't they?"

"Can I buy you a drink?"

"I don't drink." She had the most wonderful dimples when she smiled, a shy way of looking down. I almost missed it because of the piercings.

"You don't drink? My God, how do you stand it?"

That bashful smile again. "I try to keep my body clean for others."

"Really? You looked like a dirty girl to me." It was my turn to smile. Oh yes: I was flowing with the buzz, reaching into my bag of tricks. In the glow of neon beer signs it was hard to tell if she was blushing. She looked me dead in the eye:

"When you fuck me, choke me."

This was far outside the scope of my bag of tricks. I smiled politely at her and flagged the bartender to bring me another Corona. Then the lights went dim and Amanda said:

"Oh, it's time for Daryl."

We both turned to the stage. The music was lowered and a voice emanated from the darkness:

"Creatures of darkness"—honestly, this was how it began—"welcome to Purgatory!" The crowd cheered and howled. "Tonight, for your pleasure, our own Lord Moltor presents a live demonstration in which he brings a virgin over to..." there was a significant pause here "...the darkness!" The crowd howled again, and Daryl appeared on stage escorting a raven-haired woman in a white dress. I started to say something to Amanda, but the voice erupted from the P.A. system again. "I forgot to mention that Lord Moltor is a licensed phlebotomist. Please do not attempt to replicate his demonstration at home unless you are under the supervision of a healthcare professional. Thank you." Daryl—Lord Moltor—helped the woman lay back on the coffee table and he took a seat on the throne behind her. As he did so the music began again, a slow, pulsing rhythm that was deliberately aimed at heightening the dramatic tension of whatever dinner theater production they were putting on. Daryl raised the woman's arm so that her wrist faced the audience. Then he produced a scalpel and most of the crowd applauded and whistled.

I didn't want to find out if I was about to see the real deal or not. Simulated blood-letting is only slightly more appealing than the actual act, and neither ranks very high for me. Blood doesn't bother me, knives do not bother me, but when a knife is finely splitting flesh to draw out blood, I simply can't handle it. Needles impact me the same way; whenever I watch a movie and it contains a scene of someone being injected, I have to avert my eyes. I've no doubt I will die of arterial disease because a cholesterol test is far too frightening for me to face.

I leaned down to Amanda's ear; metal brushed my lips. "I need to go outside." I didn't wait for her response.

I staggered through the crowd toward the exit. It was cool outside, and I took deep gulps of air. I could feel the spit welling up in my mouth, and I stumbled into the parking lot and pressed my hands against the hood of a car to steady myself. I lay my face against the cool metal, but I heaved and threw up anyway.

"Are you okay?" It was Amanda. Her hand was on my back. I slumped against the side of the car embarrassed and incredibly inebriated. "If you want we can just go back to my place and you can rest. Maybe you had too much to drink." She had the most benevolent smile.

"That sounds nice," I said, and I wiped my mouth on the back of my sleeve. She held out her hand to help me up, and that's when I saw the raised scar on her forearm, and then I saw what it spelled: Daryl. I leaned over and puked again. And then several times more. When I looked up, Amanda was gone.

I sifted through my vomit for portions of pills, found a half of an undigested Percocet, and popped it in my mouth. I had enough post nausea salivation going on that it was easy to swallow. I reached in my pocket for my cell to call a cab, and I began to laugh. There was no reason to fear blood-thirsty vampires at all: I'd forgotten I had my rosary.

V.

It's true: for that expanse of thirteen years that blossomed between my freshman year of college and my grandfather's death, I never once prayed in earnest, save for those occasions when prayer was all that was left for me. Not that I can recall anyway. But I didn't tell you this:

When I was living in Syracuse there was an old man—he looked about 65 or so—who stood on the corner of Marshall Street and University Boulevard handing out rosaries. Regardless of the weather he was usually adorned in a jogging suit and baseball hat, and he had the beard of man just back from wandering in the wilderness. He had a duffel bag at his feet—apparently stuffed full with cheap, plastic rosaries. He didn't proselytize, nor did he even hold out a rosary to suggest that those passing by should take one from him. I would watch him from the window of No Borders, the coffee shop where I spent most of my waking hours in those days. Occasionally someone would stop and take a rosary, and some people even offered him a few dollars—he always waved it off. He appeared to have a very subtle agenda, if he even had one.

I walked past him every day for months, and each time I approached his corner I thought, *Take one! Take one! Just do it! Give the man some joy in his senseless life!* But I never had the guts. I was too afraid someone I knew would see and I would have to explain myself. Many of my friends at school were actually Marxists, determined to liberate the workers of the world, and I was not up to fending off their critique of my bourgeois theology. Or I was afraid a hot chick would see me (a fact that didn't prevent me from madly picking my nose as a drove about town) and not fuck me because she'd seen me taking a rosary. My logic was terribly imperfect.

However, one afternoon in the coffee shop I helped my friend Chad perfect his cappuccino. He poured and frothed; I sampled the results. By the time he'd mastered his technique I practically vibrated out the door. I felt ill. Something in my intestines was rapidly working its way toward an exit, and I couldn't bring myself to return to the coffee shop and use their facilities—I have a fairly strong resistance to sitting on public toilets, and I'm not adept at hovering. Also, whatever was about to happen to me, it was going to require a shower afterwards.

Considering all this, I can't really offer an adequate explanation for why I stopped and took a rosary. Violent bowel movements frighten me, I suppose.

When I took the rosary the man asked me, "Do you know what this is?"

"Yes."

He nodded and I made a mad dash for my car. It was touch and go for a few blocks, but I arrived home just in time.

I keep that rosary in my pocket when I go out. Not all the time, but I carry it to weddings, funerals, and whenever I feel like I might need a back-up plan of the supernatural sort— the latter reason being far more common than the preceding two. I don't use the rosary for its intended purpose, making the mechanical march through the beads, nor do I feel particularly protected. But if prayer is at its best a way of remembering how fragile and helpless we all are, God or no God, and making a concentrated effort to be just the least bit grateful for existence, then I have actually prayed quite frequently since the rosary passed into my hands. When I reach for my keys or some change and my knuckles brush that plastic relic, I am thankful to whatever will accept my thanks. When I open my desk drawer and see the rosary in its typical place of rest, I'm grateful for people who believe in something, however strange it may seem, and especially those serene souls who stand on street corners simply to remind us how mysterious and beautiful the world is. All the angry words that Lorraine spit at me, and if I am holding that ridiculous trinket when I think of her, none of that matters: I recall an afternoon when she and I lay in the twin bed I had when I first moved into my apartment. It was July, and a brief summer shower had swept across the city, leaving the long limbs of aging poplars and oaks dripping outside our window. We were naked, entwined, and we stayed like that for a very long time, staring into the canopy of trees that fanned out around us, and we didn't leave the bed until the sun emerged again and the earth began to steam.

Memory is the only act of faith I can manage.

* * *

When the cab dropped me off I went in through the front

door of my apartment. Normally I used the back door which connects the kitchen to the fire escape, but it was a blind turn from the kitchen into the living room, and I'd been surprised before by of one Lorraine's stealthy attacks. I wanted a little space to prepare a defense if things ended up going down that way. It seemed possible that they could. I'd been gone long enough that Lorraine had sufficient time to work herself into a good lather over something trivial.

I slid my key into the lock as quietly as possible and opened the door. It seemed to creak louder than usual, and I stepped quickly into the apartment and closed it behind me. I'd expected the crepuscular glow of the television, but everything was dark. I took a few steps and stopped. The refrigerator hummed contently in the kitchen. A cat's claws picked at the fabric of the couch, and when the cat jumped down and started toward me I heard it again. I waited for Lorraine's voice or the floor to squeak under her footsteps. When my eyes finally adjusted to the pale illumination of the room from the streetlight outside the window it made sense: things were missing, and what I was hearing was the echo of open space.

The cat began to purr in time with the refrigerator. I didn't bother to look for a note, but instead sat down and stretched out on the bare floor and thought about Lorraine. In the empty room awash with pale light, answers were beginning to take shape.

Interlude with the Vampire (Nerve Mix)*

* (And just in case you skipped ahead and missed the note on the previous version of this story, here it is again):

[Allow me for a moment to return to the subject of truth that I touched upon in the preface to this collection. The observant reader will notice that there are two versions of the story "Interlude with the Vampire" contained herein. Both are entirely true; neither is entirely true *as it is told*. I can practically hear some of you crying out, "Dirty pool!" Well, not entirely. I expect that the people reading my work—the obsessive readers, the loiterers of literature—might be wise to the fact that I like to play little games. Such is the case in one of the versions of these stories: I make it very plain which story is to be least trusted, and I do it by summoning our old friend Nathaniel Hawthorne to the party. I pose the same choice to you as he did in "Young Goodman Brown," another fellow who shared my curiosity at being out well past the hour when all decent folk have gone to bed.]

I was sitting in the sun trying to collect my thoughts before I taught my next class. Things had not been going well, and I had the constant feeling that I needed to take a nap.

My fatigue was a product of my girlfriend's temper. Her sexual talents were such that it was easy to overlook her weekly fits of alcohol induced rage: a broken television, smashed glasses, personal items dismissed from the apartment via the window.

In retrospect, the solution was simple: change the locks

and quit answering her calls. However, as much as I hate to admit it, I was genuinely afraid of this woman—and not because of the threat she posed to my more fragile possessions: she routinely smacked the shit out of *me*.

Because of my slight build, I learned early in life to extract myself from volatile situations with a quick wit, and, failing that, a pretty quick sprint. Such tactics are fairly useless against an angry woman as I discovered when Lorraine began ranting at me one night when I attended a poetry reading without her:

"I know you're just out trying to fuck someone else!" She whipped a book at my head; luckily it was *Gravity's Rainbow,* which is not at all aerodynamic. "Some fucking poetry slut!"

(Oh, if only such a slut did exist! I'd be buggering her nightly while I intoned "Ode to a Grecian Urn.")

However, I was soon getting my ass kicked several times a month. The causes of her rage are irrelevant, and quite honestly I wasn't sure of the source in most instances anyway. I bore the constant humiliation of my girlfriend slapping me around in my typical manner: I got stoned. Whatever the drawbacks of marijuana, it's good for helping one forget the recent past. Alas, one of those drawbacks is that being high and being angry cannot occur simultaneously. Thus, my remedy for her abuse amounted to, "Be cool, Lorraine, be cool. Let me put the second set of Madison Square Garden '96 on the stereo and make some nachos." It didn't take me long to figure out that if you're dealing with a psychotic girlfriend, offering to play recordings of Phish does little in the way of reducing tension.

During the days, though, I stewed with venom. I thought of men like Robert Mitchum, Humphrey Bogart. They weren't violent towards women, but by God when a woman needed straightening out they didn't hesitate at giving her a solid slap. Sometimes two, if the occasion warranted. I dreamed often of slapping Lorraine so hard that it knocked her earrings off. However, the fact that I wanted my slap to be an homage to June Allyson's bitch-slap of Joan Collins in *The Opposite Sex* gave me the impression that I was not the man for the task.

All of this was swimming in my head when one of my students sat down beside me and said:

"So, you ever had any Absinthe before?"

The comment wasn't completely random; Gary was a student in my American Literature class, and during a lecture on Hemingway I was prompted to explain a reference to Absinthe in a short story. He'd been the only other person in the room besides me who knew what it was.

I told him a friend had brought some back from Europe several years before and I'd tried it then.

"Did it fuck you up?" His tone lacked the voyeurism of indulgence one might expect; it had a palpable clinical nature to it.

"I didn't have enough."

"Well, if you ever want some, let me know; I keep it around."

"You like it that much?"

"No, it's..." Gary took a drag from his cigarette and glanced around; we were more or less alone. "I practice vampirism. It's part of a ritual."

I turned my head toward Gary: he was a stocky country boy with coal-black hair and muscles shaped by labor and not the ridiculous repetition of weights; he looked directly into my eyes, and his eyes were the color of slate. I'd gotten used to students telling me completely bizarre and personal things—people are always looking for an authority figure to heap their issues on for some shred of absolution. And even though this was quite possibly in the top three weirdo admissions of all time, I thought it best not to laugh at his confession. But it was hard to ignore the fact that I was sitting in the sun with a guy who claimed to be a vampire.

"So what's with the absinthe?" I asked.

"Oh, that. Well, you know it's potent shit. Most people it just fucks up. But it won't even intoxicate a vampire. It's a test, you know. To see if you've got the gene."

"What gene?"

"The vampire gene."

A scientific debate with someone claiming the existence of a vampire gene seemed rather pointless. I let the matter slide.

"So, do you like, you know, bite necks?"

"Do I look like I have fucking fangs to you?" He flashed his teeth.

"Uh, no."

"Yeah," and his face dropped. "It sucks. I just can't afford to have the work done. But if I could afford them, I'd have them."

I wasn't sure how to respond to this, so I sat quietly. Then Gary said:

"How old do I look to you?"

"I don't know," I said. "Twenty-five?"

"I'm thirty-eight."

"You're older than I am."

"Get yourself a woman who treats you right. You'll feel the difference in your blood." He smiled, exposing a mouthful of beautiful white teeth. "Just think about it. If you want to meet a nice girl I know the place." I wasn't sure what a vampire who attended the local community college might have in mind when he said "nice girl," but considering my own circumstances at the time I didn't need to bring any more drama into my life.

When I got home that night I made the puzzling discovery that my apartment was littered with confetti. Upon closer examination I realized the confetti was actually the pages of my journals, which Lorraine had taken great care to manufacture into fantastically small pieces. Apparently, my private thoughts about her were not to her liking. I found a note in the bathroom that read: *Fuck you, faggot.* I also found my toothbrush in the toilet.

The next day after class I asked Gary just what he meant by a "nice girl."

"Come and see for yourself. I'm going there tonight."

"Where?"

"Purgatory."

I considered this. "On a Tuesday?"

I met Gary (or rather, *Count Gary,* as I'd begun to think of him) later that night outside the bar that hosts Purgatory. I'd researched it a little on the internet that afternoon—it was a monthly gathering of the leather and S&M community. It seemed safe enough, but whenever someone admits to being a vampire and then invites you to attend a place called purgatory with them, well, I feel a background check is in order.

As we walked in, Gary put his arm around my shoulder and said, "Tonight you'll feel like a new man." The leather of his jacket creaked in my ear.

In my daily existence, I am most often dressed like a nine year-old on his way to baseball practice: Converse sneakers, jeans, and a jersey style t-shirt with the ¾ length sleeves. However, it was my leather belt that was most similar to the wardrobes of the other attendees. I was surrounded by extras

from *Interview with the Vampire*—or a Renaissance
Festival. Either way, I felt very much like the Southern
preppy in Count Gary's court. As I surveyed the room I
thought, *One or more of these people is very likely carrying
a set of twelve-sided dice.*

My mood might have tepidly approached something close
to genuine fear had we been in a place more "dungeon-
esque." However, we were at bar known for its regular
booking of tribute bands, and so a person clad in leather with
honest-to-God fangs doesn't look at all threatening standing
in front of a sign advertising 2-for-1 Jell-O shooters and
$1.50 margaritas on Fridays.

After we'd paid our $10 cover (it seemed only fitting one
should pay a nominal fee to gain entrance to Purgatory), I
followed Gary to the bar and ordered the best beer
available—a Corona for Christ's sake! Oh, Purgatory indeed!
I discreetly popped two Percocets in my mouth, crunched
them up, and washed them down with that most mediocre of
Mexican concoctions. I would have rather gone outside and
smoked a joint, but Gary didn't exude the pleasant
indifference of a weed aficionado. Besides, at the bar, he'd
ordered a Red Bull. The one time I ordered a Red Bull I was
up until five a.m. crapping a substance that I thought was a
precursor of death. That alone was proof enough for me that
people who drink that stuff are wired differently than I am.

Gary stood at such a distance from me that it was
uncertain as to whether we actually knew each other or not. I
sat on a barstool and waited for the warm bliss of the Percs
to wash over me, and watched as the medievally clad crowd
circulated and exchanged greetings. Whenever anyone saw
Gary they gave an enthusiastic wave. His reply was a terse
nod in every case. Whenever their eyes fell on me they all
appeared to snarl. I smiled politely and raised my Corona.

This went on for some time, and as no one was speaking to me—including Gary—I was soon tipping back my fifth Corona and considering a cab ride home. The Nine Inch Nails that had been pumping on the stereo since our arrival had given way to something resembling the sounds of a genocidal massacre mixed with asphalt production, and it was decidedly not conversation friendly. The scene seemed a terrible waste of a buzz, and I felt as though I were literally buzzing. Humming, in fact.

A petite girl with purple streaks in her hair and ample piercings walked over to Gary and curtsied. He smiled at her and opened his arms; when he embraced her he pressed his face into her neck. In addition to her thin black dress and dog collar, she was wearing a pair of bright white Keds that glowed under the black-lights. Gary yelled at the girl:

"This is my friend, Kevin." The veins in his neck stood out, but he was still barely audible over the music. I leaned my head close to theirs.

"Heaven?" She said.

"Kevin," Gary repeated.

"Oh." She turned to me and smiled and curtsied again.

Gary pressed his lips to my ear. "Ok, you're all set. I've got business to take care of. I'll see you later. Or maybe not." He gave me what I can only characterize as a wicked smile. I grabbed his arm before he could walk away.

"What? What? Where are you going?"

"I'm going to find something to eat. Amanda is yours for the night. I set it all up. She'll treat you right. Remember that when you're grading finals." Gary winked.

"How do you know her?"

He smiled at me again: "She's a good source of food." I let go of his arm and he pressed into the crowd. As soon as he was gone I said to Amanda:

"Can I buy you a drink?"

"I don't drink." She had the most wonderful dimples when she smiled, a shy way of looking down. I almost missed it because of the piercings.

"You don't drink? My God, how do you stand it?"

That bashful smile again. "I try to keep my body clean for others."

"Really? You looked like a dirty girl to me." It was my turn to smile. Oh yes: I was flowing with the buzz, reaching into my bag of tricks. In the glow of neon beer signs it was hard to tell if she was blushing. She looked me dead in the eye:

"When you fuck me, choke me."

This was far outside the scope of my bag of tricks. I smiled politely at her and flagged the bartender to bring me another Corona. I downed it quickly as Amanda and I smiled at each other. Occasionally she leaned into me and seemed to say something, but I couldn't hear a word over the music. I smiled and nodded, and that seemed to be working fine. When I was done with my beer I jerked my thumb toward the door, and she and I walked out into the warm night.

"So what's the plan, Amanda?"

"What do you want it to be?" She didn't say it with the flirtatious sarcasm of a sorority girl, but with the submissive tone of someone who genuinely wants to please.

"Well you mentioned the matter of choking..." The way I said it sounded oddly Victorian, but regardless I felt the signs were pretty clear: Gary had set this up, she knew the deal, and it seemed stupid to stand around acting as though the night wasn't going end up like this anyway. At least once or twice in my life I've stumbled into easy hookups like this and have been smart enough to latch on. Conversely, I've managed to fuck things up about two dozen times or more.

Probably more. I try not to dwell on superlatives in matters of failure.

Her impish smile blossomed into a fierce seriousness:

"You can do what you want with me, but do it hard, and drink me up."

As hammered as I was I recall thinking: *Do people really talk like this?* But then I remembered the scene inside: the gothic aesthetic, the people who clearly thought The Gimp was the best character in *Pulp Fiction*. At this point everything was beginning to seem like a dream, and oh yes, this little girl standing in front of me was begging to be hurt, and I wanted to hurt someone just as badly as I'd been hurting lately.

"Well, Amanda—" the thought passed through my head that this girl and my mother shared the same name "—where are you parked?"

Curiously, her apartment did not bear the stony coldness of a bourgeois succubus' lair, decked out in crystals and dragons and fairies, but appeared instead to be a showroom for Pier 1; she had an amazing collection of throw pillows.

As soon as we were in the door she was on me: she was small, maybe 100 pounds, and it felt effortless to have her clinging to me, legs wrapped around my waist. Normally I don't feel very manly when having sex with a woman: I feel like a beetle clinging to a lioness. But her tiny body made me feel enormous; I could have crushed her. We fell amongst the throw pillows, her hands working my clothes from me with professional ease, and as her tongue worked its way into my mouth I felt not one but two studs in her tongue. Oh, sweet bliss! I nearly swooned right then imagining what mysteries her metallic mouth might unleash.

She hiked up her dress and said, "Spank my ass."

I complied with her request. I was never one to turn down a little ass chapping. But with each smack of my hand she said, "Harder!" Within a few swats my hand was hurting—it reminded me of playing baseball as a kid, the way the wooden bat stung your hands and wrists when it connected with the ball. It seemed I couldn't hit her hard enough and this was beginning to piss me off. I reached up and grabbed the dog collar from behind, yanking backwards as her teeth latched onto my lips; I pulled harder and she came loose from me, splitting my lower lip as she did so.

"Ack!" I said, and as she straddled me with her head pulled back by the collar, she ran her tongue across her lips and smiled: that's when I caught a good glimpse of the fangs, tipped with the slightest bit of my blood, and before I could say anything she said:

"Wait right here."

The warning signals in my brain were at Def-Con One: *Get the fuck out of here.* But I had lapsed into an opiated euphoria, and I began to imagine her as my vampish girlfriend and how her throw pillows and accent rugs would blend seamlessly into my own apartment and my menagerie of colored glass votives. And Lorraine—she'd quit screwing with me if I had a new girlfriend with fangs.

"I've brought you something special." I opened my eyes; Amanda was holding out a drink to me; her other hand held a shimmering light, and when I sat up to take the drink I saw it was knife.

Well, so this is how it ends, I thought. I don't know if I was completely twisted or what, but I felt unusually calm—all my problems were about to disappear as I became the victim of some serial killer. It was really quite liberating.

Then she handed the knife to me.

"You don't have to be gentle," she said, and she began to

peel off her clothing, and on one wrist I saw the single needled tattoo of a razor blade, and on the other wrist the tattoo that read 'cut here,'--the words floated above a dotted line; a mummified kitten was stenciled onto her stomach and chest. (I have to admit I found this somewhat charming as I own ten cats, and I had to repress the urge to say, "Oh, a little kitty..."). But nearly every inch of her skin bore some scar—some looked like memories of girlhood boredom and hate; others had a pink newness as though recently born.

She sat beside me on the couch, kissing me with that slight bite, and guided my hand with the knife toward her thigh. I could feel the blackness beginning even then, as if a small pinhole had opened in the back of my head letting all the anger and resentment I'd been hording about the circumstances of my life float into the night, and I was beginning to feel light and empty.

"Taste me," she breathed, and I felt her hand pressing against mine, guiding the knife lightly along her leg; I looked down and saw the thread of crimson appear. "I'm pure," she said. As I raised my head to look at her the scar across her chest very clearly spelled something. I was leaning closer to look—the lights were going out fast, but I swear the raised letters spelled 'Gary'.

I've never been much for blood—mine or anyone else's. My annual physicals as a child were something of a nightmare for all involved as I was (and still remain) quick to faint at the mere sight of a needle or blood being drawn from someone's body. Even a visit to the dentist presents serious obstacles as a shot of Novocain not only numbs me, it puts me into a coma. You know my dentist has a high regard for my masculinity when he tells me at the beginning of an appointment that the cool rags are ready and waiting for when I inevitably come around.

When I came around from the vampyress' sweet embrace I woke to sunlight. I was sitting on the couch, fully clothed. No one seemed to be in the apartment but me. Had I fallen asleep and only dreamed a wild meeting with a vampire? Be it so, if you will; I didn't stick around to find out, but instead made a hasty exit and found my car. When I looked in the rear-view mirror I saw the cuts on my lower lip.

It occurred to me that Lorraine would have driven by my apartment last night; she would have noticed my absent car, perhaps even waited for me. I could not begin to guess what loss I was about to return to, but I felt it prudent to stop on the way home and purchase a new toothbrush.

Swing Town

A few months after I'd broken up with Lorraine, she sent this text message to my cell phone: *I just want u 2 know I slept w/ Brian while u &I were still dating. That's right, we had sex. Revenge is a dish best served cold.*

She actually said that thing about revenge-- I wish that were some terrible cliché that bubbled up from my poor imagination, but instead it's a terrible cliché from a woman with whom I had sex for three years. For quite a while I was unsure whether it was the content of her message or the phrasing that upset me most. She had a real chance to say something that would have tipped the spear of her confession with a more potent poison, something like, *His cock was the solution to the riddle of our relationship.* Certainly it's not Shakespeare, but it would have confused me for months.

Brian was a friend who lived across the street, a trusted companion, and a devout Christian. That last item should have raised a red flag immediately that he was going to cause trouble. I should know: I was raised in the church in the South, and since you're taught that humans are eternally flawed and Jesus forgives no matter what, those that buy into the programming are more or less free to screw up as much as they like and never serve any real time in eternal damnation. All that limits you is your ability to negotiate the gauntlet of consequences in *this* world-- a skill at which most folks are rather adept.

But because Brian kept a supply of premium hash in his apartment it was for this reason that I was willing to let my instincts take a backseat along with my consciousness. (I have my beliefs, too, and getting really high whenever possible is at the top of my commandments.) Truthfully, though, I couldn't have cared any less that Brian had nailed Lorraine, despite the fact that he never told me about it and that I was sleeping a mere 10 feet away when it happened. Lorraine was in the past, and so any vengeance or betrayal that involved her was a moot point. Besides, she and Brian and I had spent the night drinking and joking around about the possibility of a three-way, but because of all the hash I became narcoleptic rather early; Lorraine was a horny beast when she drank and I knew that. What ultimately pissed me off was the realization that, once again, my dream of group sex had come so very close to fulfillment, but instead of orgiastic ecstasy I am left only with the memory of a sweet, solitary slumber. Story of my life.

Actually, my dream would have only been *grazed* rather than satiated had I been a participant in Lorraine and Brian's copulation. My ideal situation would have involved me and two women. At one time this seemed like an achievable objective, and I approached it with cold, military calculation. It was a two-pronged attack that involved the initial recruitment of an ally (my friends who had fallen upon the good fortune to engage in a threesome always implied that bringing in that key third element was easier if you already had one woman with you), followed by a joint campaign of invading a willing lass of our choosing. My mistake was always trying to form a pact with my current girlfriend, and few questions shake the foundation of a woman's self esteem like, "Hey, honey, how about we bring another woman into bed with us? You know, just for kicks..."

It was also my misfortune to constantly date women who had already been through this experience. Whenever I began a new relationship and the inevitable cataloging of each other's romantic résumé commenced (an activity that is most often accompanied by a late hour and many drinks), it was the *ménage à trois* category that gave me the most heartache. If my girlfriend had participated in group sex before, it was usually framed in this manner, "Me and [insert female name here] and our friend [insert male name here] were really fucked up one night, and it just happened... It's not something I'd do with someone I was actually *dating*. That just wouldn't work, you know?" I always asserted that I, as a point of fact, *didn't know*, but that I was willing to test those waters because that's how one gains knowledge. How could anyone really and truly know how they felt about watching their partner have sex with someone else unless they had tried it? Besides, translated literally from the French, ménage à trois means "household for three." Granted, it means "three people fucking" in English, but isn't there some wisdom in the literal French, some nuanced notion that invokes the trinity and implies that we are all God's creatures, that we should live (and fuck) together in perfect harmony, that we are all one in this house of a world?

Had I been dating Aristotle I've no doubt my argument would have been viewed as the epitome of rational thinking and certainly been put to the test. (Then again, a Greek guy will go along with just about anything to get laid.) But regardless of whether or not my girlfriends had previously dipped their toes in the orgy-pool, my attempts at getting them to sign on to such a tempting treaty were always met with the same dismissive laugh and look which said, *Hey pal, you're lucky to be getting what you're getting-- don't push it.*

It occurred to me that I could take things on alone and attempt to be one of those lucky lads who happens to fall into bed one drunken/stoned night with two of his female friends, but there was an immediate obstacle that made the task more Herculean than it might normally be: I have few female friends, particularly those that are available for group sex. I tend to have more emotionally satisfying and comfortable relationships with men, and if I have a friendship with a woman it's usually because she has some quality that I find attractive, and when a woman possesses such a quality, I want to have sex with her. Thus, I have more ex-girlfriends than genuine female companions, and I would endeavor to put my time towards dismantling Mount Rushmore with 19th century dental tools rather than endure the agony of trying to coax one or two of them back into bed with me. As to the matter of approaching two women previously unknown to me about the prospect of a three-way: rejection from one woman was dreadful enough; why double-down on humiliation?

However, at the beginning of my relationship with Lorraine when we reached that point where it was necessary to tally the failures of our past loves and detail those desires which delighted us, her stance on the three-way was not the traditional response I'd grown accustomed to. While she admitted to a single incident of the sort in her own past (an unpleasant event, as she described it, involving a great deal of cocaine, her sister's ex-boyfriend and a cherubic stripper named Poppy), she didn't rule out any future experiences. Her exact phrasing was, "Put a ring on my finger and I'll do whatever you want."

This was the beginning of a series of statements that should have activated the air-raid sirens in my brain, but the blitz was already underway: Lorraine was just stunningly beautiful and fucked like a cat with its tail stuck in an electrical socket. Although she would eventually get around to throwing a blistering hot espresso on me, smashing my

television, and chasing me around my apartment with a
loaded Red Ryder BB gun (I abandoned all pretense of
masculinity that night-- I wasn't about to lose an eye to
demonstrate I was as cool under fire as Bugs Bunny), I
dismissed these events simply as proof that her love for me
was deeply passionate, however oddly she might choose to
express it. I am a shallow man; I liked having a beautiful
girlfriend, and the television needed replacing anyway.

Over the ensuing months I would broach the subject of
group activities, and Lorraine's answer was always the same:
buy her a ring and she'd be my willing slave. The dilemma
would have been easily resolved, I think, for most men, but I
didn't want a willing slave; I wanted a willing partner. On the
flip side, I had no desire for a wife. A hot girlfriend was one
thing, but a wife-- a wife involved legally binding contractual
arrangements, and I have an intense aversion to any
situation which does not afford me the comfort of a quick
and hassle-free exit.

Other than her occasional psychotic outbursts and
statements ("If you ever try to leave me I will call all your
friends and tell them how much you hate them and that you
used to beat me" which she actually did, but not because I
tried to leave her; she did it because I wouldn't buy her a
hairless cat-- I have eight cats, and I was more than willing to
shave one), my only other grievance with Lorraine was that
she loved holidays. I love holidays, too, but I also like being
in bed at a reasonable hour. This is mainly due to the fact
that I like smoking pot, and the side effect is that after
giggling at everything for a while, I become hungry, then
extremely sleepy. Lorraine was a serious weekend and
holiday drinker, and if you've been around such folks you
know quite well their capacity for stretching their decadence
into the early hours of the next morning. I have little

tolerance for such behavior, perhaps because I do not understand the binge mentality: why cram everything into one night and feel like shit for the next day or two, when you can stretch that pleasure moderately across the whole week?

Thus, when it came to parties and other late night social activities, I was quite content to let Lorraine go with her friends while I sat at home and listened to my old Michael Jackson records, occasionally calling up my friend Chad to say, *Listen to the funk in "Rock with You"* as I turned the volume up on the stereo so that it might be audible over the telephone.

After one of these parties in early December 2003, at which I was not present, Lorraine returned with an invitation to yet another soirée on New Year's Eve. This party was right around the corner from my apartment, and it took place at the home of a former Maybelline model turned dental hygienist and her boyfriend.

"How do you know these people?" I asked.

"She's my dental hygienist."

Being around people in the dental trade makes me uncomfortable as it is; I have an incisor that was chipped by an errant Frisbee during a game of disc golf, and I always feel like they're looking at my teeth. Also, I don't have a good relationship with New Year's Eve-- it's been a let down my whole life, and I find a good night's rest for myself far more pleasing than putting another year of the same old shit to bed. I told Lorraine I'd probably just sit at home and try to decide on the ultimate rock vocalist: it was down to Roger Daltry or David Lee Roth, but I didn't know how much credit to give Elvis for being the first.

Lorraine frowned and walked out of the room. I was prepared for the sound of one of my more valuable possessions hitting the ground, but instead Lorraine re-emerged from the bedroom, nude, and said, "They're swingers." Then she proceeded to remove my cock from my pants, suck it a little, spit on it, and place it between her scrumptious breasts which she pumped up and down on my shaft until I heard the assailing, triumphant yell of Roger Daltry from "Won't Get Fooled Again" reverberate through my head.

Prior to the invitation to the New Year's swingers' party, the closest I'd come to a group encounter happened via the phone. I do not refer to the party phonesex lines that I called with impunity in my youth and beyond, but to a curious period in my relationship with Bridget, back when I was still in graduate school.

Bridget was bisexual, but fiercely monogamous, and so her desire to involve anyone else in our lovemaking was as nonexistent as that desire had been with previous girlfriends. However, Bridget had experienced the pleasure of another woman, and it is simply a fact of the universe that one female can provide for another what a man never can. What it is that's provided I've no clue; as I lack a vagina I hesitate to speak for those who possess one. But having a cock, I can say something about the psychology of that thing: it is just that-- a *thing*. It dangles from one's body like a gregarious dog on a minuscule leash, constantly nosing ahead of its owner, always wanting to be petted or scratched, getting into things it shouldn't get into, making a mess. Or it is a mildly useful tool, often a good gauge on just how cold it is wherever you're standing at the moment, or it functions nicely as a novelty towel rack for moderate amounts of time. (I've heard that some men can open a beer bottle with their penis, but I can neither imagine the mechanics of such a feat nor the desire to attempt it.) It is an entity at once attached and yet separate from you. As far as I know, every implement of war bears some resemblance to a testicle or a penis, and that should tell you something right there: the masculine aspect lacks a tenderness, a capacity for acceptance.

My personal encounter with Bridget's strap-on dildo had taught me my own limits of acceptance, and while I knew that she would not stomach the idea of me having sex with her and a strange girl, I suspected she might miss the sound of a woman coming, and so I proposed the idea of she and I having sex while we talked with a girl on the phone.

There was little, if any, hesitation to her answer: "Well, where do we find this girl?"

"Online."

Bridget began to peel off her clothes. "Get to it."

I discovered that finding a woman to have phonesex with me and my girlfriend was much easier than finding a woman to have phonesex with just me. I conjecture this is due to the high volume of single men who congregate on the internet in search of phonesex with a woman who is into the act altruistically; a man who already has a woman with him is less likely to be a loser or a stalker (in most cases), and besides it's often more entertaining to listen to a couple have sex than a man masturbate.

Our first few encounters with various women presented certain obstacles, the biggest one being the most efficient way to fuck while holding the phone. Alas, as college students we could neither afford a headset nor a speakerphone, and had to make do with a bulky cordless unit I'd inherited from my grandparents. The best position depended on who was doing the talking: if I was on the phone, then it was doggy-style (a descriptive term I have loathed since I was a teenager, as so many more interesting animals have sex in this position, though "goat-style" implies a satanic filthiness about the act), and if it was Bridget then it was missionary on her riding me.

While it wasn't a part of our regular sexual routine, when the occasion presented itself (usually when my roommate Steve was absent, which was not often) the added thrill of some anonymous woman masturbating to the sounds and descriptions of our love making (Bridget and I, as baseball fans, were pretty good at giving a detailed play-by-play of what was happening) heightened the intensity of our orgasms. I often had to restrain myself from a quick release, and I couldn't imagine the even greater pleasure that must certainly be a part of genuine, physical group sex. I was fairly sure at that time in my life that should an opportunity arise it wouldn't be worth it: my anticipation would be so excessive that I'd go off like a geyser just prior to earth-shattering seismic activity.

As all earthly delights, the phone three-ways did not have an infinite shelf life. The end came during a session with a girl Bridget and I had spoken to several times. We had paused to switch positions, and when Bridget handed the phone to me the girl on the other end said, "Is that Phish playing the background?" Indeed, it was Phish, and as Phish is one of those breeds of bands that inspire a tedious fanaticism in their listeners, the girl and I launched into a painfully intricate discussion of the various shows we had been to, what we thought of the new songs they were playing, and the peak performances of the last ten years. While this conversation actually made my cock even harder than it already was, Bridget was not amused in the least. She finally snatched the receiver from my hands, hung up on our phonesex partner, dressed silently and walked back to her apartment. I didn't bring the subject up again.

In the weeks before New Year's Eve, I pestered Lorraine with questions about our hosts. Mainly these questions related to the hotness factor of Lorraine's hygienist, and then minor queries such as, "What does one wear to a swingers' house?" My wardrobe is limited-- mainly a menagerie of clothes that ex-girlfriends have bought me because I apparently lack the ability to attire myself in an acceptable manner-- and there was the potential to have sex with a former Maybelline model. Or any other number of women, for all that I knew. I wanted to be dressed as appropriately and desirably as possible. Lorraine was vague on the particulars of my own clothing choices, but certain that the party would be large, intense, and fantastic, and attended by folks in casual evening wear. That made the decision easy for me: khaki pants, white shirt-- my standard dress for events that fall between the casualness of playing horseshoes and the formality of funerals.

Any other questions regarding the party I tended to ask in the bedroom while Lorraine and I were fucking, and these were repetitive questions along the lines of, "You like this dick don't you? But it's not enough is it? You want more than one cock, don't you?" Often Lorraine shouted her answers, most usually, "Give me two dicks! I want another fucking cock in my mouth!"

As I live in a building that was built in 1949, the insulation between apartments doesn't absorb sounds as it might in a more modern dwelling, and after these late night Q&A fucking sessions, my downstairs neighbor, Jennifer, would level a curious gaze at me when we inevitably ran into each other the following day. She never said anything about it at the time, but at a cookout at our apartment some months later when Lorraine stated that she only wanted one hotdog, Jennifer tilted her head and said, "Are you sure you don't want *two*? I thought you might prefer *two*." I moved my bed to the opposite end of the apartment that night.

Lorraine's spirited cries for extra dick should have been another red flag waving furiously in my face, and perhaps this accounts a little more for my lack of surprise concerning her revelation about my neighbor, Brian. Her responses were never as enthusiastic when I probed her desires to go down on her hygienist, or watch me as I viciously plunged into another woman's aching pussy. (And oh, how these things were heavy upon my mind in that interval of weeks leading up to the year's end! Every fantasy I'd conjured about the transformative alchemy of two women entwined around my body played continually in my imagination-- all those orgasms that seemed so intense when Bridget and I shared them with others via wires and satellites were about to be replaced in memory with the genuine intensity of human static, heat, and breath. I found myself masturbating with increased frequency, to the point where I eventually tore the skin on my insatiable penis-- instead of stopping I simply continued jerking off with Neosporin and hoped for the best.)

The one question I wanted to ask but avoided in the weeks prior to the party regarded the amending of Lorraine's engagement ring clause: why had she suddenly dropped this as a requirement for our mutual exploration of group sex? I didn't touch the issue; I played it as cool as I possibly could, given the fact that fulfillment of a lifelong dream was but a short time away. Also, I was happy to have the ring subject dropped *period*, regardless of its relation to swinging. In the preceding months, Lorraine had been dropping hints relentlessly that what she wanted more than anything else in this world for Christmas was an engagement ring. A lot of this pressure emanated from her mother, a Charlotte socialite who adhered to the quaint notion that a girl was destined to be an old maid if she wasn't wed by the age of twenty-five. Lorraine was teetering on the brink of spinsterhood, and thus sales flyers for jewelry stores were not carted to the recycle bin with the rest of the papers; if we were watching television and a commercial for a jewelers came on, she'd make a comment along the lines of, "That's a pretty ring-- that's the sort of ring *I'd like*." Even if she were in another room when the advertisements commenced, she would step into the doorway for the duration *just in case* a commercial featuring engagement rings came on. Perhaps she thought she was being subtle, but it's difficult to fail to notice that someone only provides commentary when a specific piece of jewelry flashes on the screen; it was a Pavlovian response to be marveled at, which I would have had I not been the target of her programming.

Besides, even if I had the desire to be married, I certainly didn't have the money; I taught college part-time, and that was enough to eek out an existence for me. I'm a terrible wage earner in the same way I've always been a poor athlete: I don't see why I should work hard to own a home and drive a nice car or the point of winning any sort of game when we're all just going to end up dead anyway. Why bother? Better to spend your time like Thoreau, working as little as possible and doing as much of what you like while you're here. Such an attitude prevents one from accumulating the capital necessary to purchase precious metals, but it does afford the luxury of acquiring a gift card to Target, and as Lorraine was soon to be moving into a new apartment I thought that a gift with the possibility for fulfilling a variety of desires was a splendid idea.

When New Year's Eve arrived I spent most of the day

restraining myself from masturbating. I was fully healed by
then and eager to avoid another friction injury-- no one
wants to expose their penis for the first time at a swingers
party and have it looking mangled and distressed. But also
my aversion to wanking was because when I am anticipating
excitement and adventure I become far to eager prior to the
event and wear myself out before anything actually happens.
This behavior doesn't confine itself merely to erotic
encounters (oh, the number of dates I've canceled at the last
minute because I've spent a whole day jerking off and thus
satisfied my hunger single-handedly!), but spills over into a
variety of social activities. I am the fellow who arrives at the
party already intoxicated, or who gets too high before the
concert. In either case, I end up sleeping through the
pinnacle of everyone else's evening, which is yet another
reason I prefer to remain in my own domicile: rarely do I
miss anything exciting by passing out early there. A cat may
knock over a fish bowl and the glass will shatter me back to
consciousness, but that's about it.

However, I did allow myself to discharge one round in the
morning and the afternoon to ensure that I wasn't overly
primed when the stars aligned later in the night. In both
instances I was watching gang-bang porn, trying to pick up
any last-minute pointers for group etiquette, but the weeks
of anticipation made me quick on the draw, and I was unable
to glean anything new. It just looked like an animalistic, free-
for-all fuck-fest. There seemed to be little actual protocol, but
these were professionals I was watching: I viewed the people
I would be meeting that night as hobbyists, and just as other
amateur groups have unwritten codes for behavior (for
instance, you can't just go groping female Klingons at the
Trekkie conventions-- I learned that the hard way), I was
certain there were policies of which I was unaware that

would complicate matters for me. But still, no matter my anxiety over the rules of order, nothing could dampen my spirits, for very soon (it was so close I could taste it) I would be having sex with two women (or more!) simultaneously.

Lorraine and I started out the door around nine that night to walk to the party; winter is often non-existent in North Carolina, and so the evening was only mildly chilly. We ambled casually through the streets of my neighborhood, the houses brightly lit with the trappings of Christmas that would be dismantled by the end of the week. Over the rooftops, through the naked winter branches, the skyline of Charlotte loomed with its imposing phallus, the Bank of America tower. Any other night I'd wish for the warm Spring rains and greening of trees to erase its presence on the horizon, but for once it looked merely like an enormous steel Christmas tree topped with a crown of stars, beaming down the last rays of the year onto the churches and shops and people below.

As we turned the corner I put my hand on Lorraine's ass; she was wearing a black cocktail dress that made her look especially fuckable. A voice from a passing car yelled, "Woohoo!" and then that car stopped just ahead of us. I recognized it: it was my brother's.

He rolled down the passenger's side window and said: "What up, dude? I thought I'd missed you."

I leaned down and put my head in the car. "We just got started," I said. "Some friends of Lorraine's are having a party."

"Cool, I was hoping you had something planned."

I turned my head to look at Lorraine; she'd lit a cigarette and was giving me the wide-eyed stare of, *No, absolutely no way is he coming*. I put my head back in the car. "I don't know, dude. You may not be dressed properly." My brother was sporting shorts, a tie-dyed t-shirt, sandals and a thick hemp necklace. He was and still is a bearded and hairy fellow.

"What the fuck, man? It's tradition that we spend New Year's together."

This was not exactly true. My brother and I had spent the previous New Year's Eve together, but that was it. It was his habit to declare anything that had occurred once a tradition if he wanted to do it again. This was not some weird revisionist history that he deployed as a way to imbue one with guilt and get his way; he was not as clever as our mother in that regard. He was being sincere, and it was for this reason that I looked back at Lorraine and made an apologetic face while simultaneously fighting the urge to grab my bother's keys from the ignition and hurl them into the bushes and take off running with Lorraine. But she had heels on, and Brandon was, after all, my younger brother. I opened the car door for her and he drove us the few blocks to Karen and Harry's.

In retrospect I could have told him, *No*. But it's not quite that simple. Though my brother has a history of intruding at the most inopportune times-- and this was certainly one of them-- I felt honor-bound to take him along even on those occasions when his presence was guaranteed to be a disaster. Though he has since moved to Arizona to be as far from our mother as possible, at this time he was still living (at the age of 24) in the same bedroom he had lived in since he was ten. Sadly, the décor had undergone few changes in those years, though he had scaled back his shrine to Star Wars after I introduced him to smoking pot-- something had to be done, and cannabis was the only remedy I could think of for a fellow who was bordering on a life of celibacy.

Part of the problem was that my brother was just entering

puberty when my mother was undergoing her first in a series of debilitating depressions. I was mostly absent during a lot of this, being older and away at college, but the fallout of her episodes easily reached me-- my father and brother were present for the meltdowns. I'm uncertain as to the particulars concerning those years, but as my father escaped into the church, my brother surfaced from adolescence absent of any discernible ambition in life, withdrawn and something of an emotional literalist: though capable of sarcasm himself, he tended to stay on the surface of meaning where others were concerned. Such traits made him vulnerable to people who took advantage of his good nature (I was shamefully among those cretins from time to time), and thus, as he was my only sibling, I had a conscience which compelled me to guardedly usher him through as many of life's experiences as possible. It would only strike me after he'd gone to Arizona that I was hovering over him exactly as my mother had done, but in a considerably different manner.

Because of my brother's inherent sincerity, he did not pickup on Lorraine's clear displeasure with his arrival during the brief ride in the car; she masked her mood with a smile and small talk, but it was conversation which meant, *Motherfucker, if I had a time machine, I would travel back to the night of your conception and convince your father to wear a condom.* I assumed this had a lot to do with the nature of the party, and I was with her in that regard: I had no desire to witness my brother have sex, or have him watch me. Or be in the same room naked with him. Or put my penis where his penis has been. There was a whole range of reasons, but I was only partially right in my speculations as to Lorraine's irritation. She knew what I did not: one of those unspoken rules I'd wondered about dictated that if there was a guy, he had to bring a girl. Single men were an unwanted nuisance.

I should have known this-- I try to enforce a very similar rule when hosting large social gatherings myself: for the heterosexual male, there's no kind of party more terrible than a sausage party. Straight men who are lubing themselves with alcohol become dangerously restless when they do not have women around to impress. In a situation where the men outnumber the women by large numbers, the males turn on one another like hungry jackals, thus ruining the mating chances of the entire herd. I fully understood the need for a delicate balance in the sexual ecosystem. But this was my brother. Surely he would have special privileges, and besides it was New Year's Eve. Where was the holiday spirit?

Karen and Harry lived in a modest cottage in the Plaza-Midwood neighborhood, just across the railroad tracks and down past the Penguin restaurant. We appeared to be the early arrivals as the house did not give off the appearance of being in full swing. Harry answered the door, a fellow roughly the same age as me, with dark hair and a chiseled, gymnast look. He was wearing roughly the same clothing as my brother.

"Lorraine!" he exclaimed as he opened the door. He pulled her into a tight embrace and kissed her full on the lips. I thought this was a bit inappropriate, swinger or not, when he suddenly released Lorraine and swept into a deep bear hug, kissing both of my cheeks and saying, "And you must be Kevin! It's so good to meet you-- Karen and I have heard so much about you." When he let me go he was beaming with a warm friendly smile, but there was something *too friendly* about it that made me uneasy. His smile quickly collapsed into puzzlement when I stepped aside and my brother, who had been loitering in the background on the front porch, moved to make his way in the house.

"And you are...?" Harry trailed off.

"Oh, I'm sorry," I said. "This is my brother, Brandon." I offered no further explanation, and Harry stuck his head out the door and glanced both ways.

"Just the three of you?"

"Yep," I said. I looked around for Lorraine; she had disappeared.

"Ah, okay. Well..." Harry stuck out his hand to my brother. "Nice to have you Brandon. Come in and have a beer."

My brother said, "Cool," but I had distinctly detected in Harry's tone that it was not cool at all. Not by a long shot.

Harry and Karen's home seemed like one catalog photo after another: every item in every room seemed carefully chosen and placed. It did not feel like an actual home, but rather a model of what the home of a 21st century, young, urban, professional couple should look like. When Harry opened the refrigerator, I noticed everything inside of it seemed arranged: things lined up in an unnatural way. The beers were in rows; the cottage cheese, sour cream, and cream cheese were placed in order of descending size. There was a menagerie of anonymous Tupperware containers also separated by size. The condiments in the refrigerator door: sized. There was a time in my life when such tidiness would have made me feel as though I had encountered my soul mates, but there was something fucked up about neat-freak swingers.

I mentioned to Harry how nice his house was, but he dismissed the comment as though he'd heard it all before, saying only, "Yeah, it's okay. Karen decorates. You guys want a bong hit?" He opened the freezer and took out three-quart size mason jars, then reached into the cupboard and removed an ornate bong standing about 18 inches high. My uneasiness began to subside significantly.

"So what we got here," Harry said as he opened the jars, "is AK-47, Trinity, and Northern Lights. What you want to start with?"

Start with? Harry had just announced he had three varieties of high grade weed-- weed that had a *name*. When marijuana has a name, prepare for the complete annihilation of reason. I consider myself a cultured smoker of pot, but I don't have the connections to rendezvous with the contraband Harry presented as though it were merely a series of frozen dinners. I was worried that I might not even remember the impending orgy.

Harry packed a sample of each variety for me and my brother, and as we worked our way through each numbing hit I heard the laughter of women emanating from a doorway. Occasionally their tittering was punctuated by a deeper voice, and I said to Harry, "Who else is here?"

"Greg and Brittany. Lorraine is probably downstairs with them and Karen."

"Oh, so we're not the first to arrive."

"Nope, you're last. I guess that makes you *it*." Harry winked at me and then put the bong to his mouth as he filled it with smoke and inhaled. My brother smiled at me.

"Last? Isn't anyone else coming?"

Harry exhaled as he spoke, making his voice sound strained. "No, it's just the six of us-- well," he titled his head toward my brother as he looked at me, "seven. We like to keep these things, you know, intimate." He winked at me again, then began packing up the bong for another round; my legs and arms tingled. I felt like I needed to speak or I would forget how to talk, so I did my best to make cocktail chatter:

"So Lorraine tells me that Karen's a hygienist; what do
you do?"

"I work at the bank. B of A."

"Cool. What do you do there?"

"I market credit cards and high-interest loans to families
and individuals who have a history of managing their debt
while accumulating more revolving accounts. It's a lucrative
market for banking right now, because so many workers--
particularly low-wage earners-- are conscientious, you
know? We market to *pride*. That's a really fresh market.
What do you do?"

"I teach."

"Tough market. Teachers are a high credit risk-- tough for
them to work more than one job to cover the bills, you
know?" He turned to my brother, "You?"

"I live at home."

"Loyalty. Good market. Parents are good about picking
up the tab. You have a credit card?"

"I use my dad's." My brother's unflinching honesty about
his dependent situation at the age of twenty-four
embarrassed me, most likely because it had been only too
recently that I was equally dependent on our parents' good
graces, and I was much older.

Harry handed the bong to me as he addressed my
brother, "Think about getting your own. If your dad banks
with us we can tie your card into his account and you'll never
have to worry about the bills with the bank-- you two can
work out some arrangement." After passing my brother the
bong, Harry said, "Well, let's go downstairs. That's where the
real party is." And then as an afterthought to my brother,
"Remind me to give you my card before you leave to give to
your dad; I'll get you both a better interest rate." My brother
nodded with sincerity.

The downstairs of Karen and Harry's house looked precisely what the basement of a swinger's house should look like: it had a large leather sofa, a recliner, a large screen television, a bar, and a bean bag chair. The lighting was dim and there was a glass top coffee table that operated as a buffet for lines of cocaine.

Lorraine was downstairs as Harry had suggested; she was sitting next to a brunette who was wearing jeans and a tank-top. Another couple-- a guy who looked similar to Harry (chiseled, athletic) and a thin, doll-like blond-- were standing at the bar. Everyone stopped talking when we got to the bottom of the steps.

"Well, the gang's all here," said Harry, and walked off to the bar to make a drink. My brother and I stood in the room, everyone staring us. My perception of time was warped, so it seemed like several minutes passed before I raised my hand and said:

"Hi, I'm Kevin." I jerked my thumb at my brother. "This is my brother." I looked at my brother; he grinned at the room. I added, "Brandon. That's his name."

The brunette stuck her hand out toward me; I had to take a few steps forward in order to reach it. "Hi Kevin," she said. "I'm Karen." When she smiled it was sheer radiance. It was easy to see why she'd been a model; she exuded a classic beauty, somewhat like Audrey Hepburn. I smiled back, lips tightly sealed, self-conscious about my chipped tooth; it probably looked as though I were attempting to stifle a fart.

The other couple introduced themselves as Greg and Brittany. Greg was in advertising; Brittany was a catalog model. (Yes, indeed, sweet God in heaven, TWO models!) They both had perfect teeth, but when Brittany smoked it sounded as though she had just inhaled a balloon full of cigarette smoke and helium.

After the introductions, everyone went back to what they were doing: conversing and pretending as though my brother and I weren't there. Harry was surveying the drink he had just made, and Brandon and I clung close to him at the bar. He said, "You two want a beer?" We did, and as he handed me mine, he said in a low voice, "You know, I think we have a lot in common."

"Yeah?" I said.

"Yeah, Lorraine's told me and Karen about you. But, you know, when we start getting naked, your brother has to hang upstairs. Nothing personal."

"It's cool. He'll be all right."

"Cool. Let's do some blow." And with that he slapped me on my back and made his way across the room to the coffee table.

Perhaps I am a bit of a prude where cocaine is concerned, but I have little tolerance for its use. This could be viewed as a hypocritical stance from a person who believes, as the late Bill Hicks did, that smoking marijuana should not only be legal but mandatory. It is not because I buy into any of the propaganda about cocaine's negative effects-- the government rarely tells the children of cocaine's wonderful use as a topical anesthetic, and that long ago the FDA approved a process of refining cocaine in a lab so that it could safely be sold to optometrists for use in ocular surgeries. But the recreational user's cocaine doesn't come from a lab; it comes (usually) from Columbia where it is a commodity that funds a terrible war and murderous gangsters. People most certainly die in the process of shipping that stuff to our shores, and that seems like some serious negative karma to be shoving up your nose.

Conversely, my weed comes from Morganton, North

Carolina, and that money keeps the small family farms of many of my fellow North Carolinians in business, as the corporate agra-structures continue to annihilate a profession that is the very foundation of human culture. My purchase of illegal homegrown marijuana also keeps, however indirectly, valuable federal dollars flowing into our severely under funded local police so they can fight the even greater problems of methamphetamine labs, domestic violence, and theft.

Of course, how any of this is more or less ethical than buying prescription drugs from corporations who withhold live-saving medicines from impoverished African nations is a matter worthy of debate. One must draw a personal line somewhere in the shifting sands of morality, and my line comes after group sex, weed, and Valium, but before cocaine, murder, and the recording career of Michael Bolton.

Thus, the party happening downstairs was minus two participants: me and my brother; Lorraine liked her coke on holidays (another point of contention between us), and I'd quietly explained to Harry that I was taking Brandon upstairs to give him the lowdown what the deal was for the night, but it gave me a worthy excuse to escape a scene with which I was uncomfortable. True, all the hot women were down there, snorting lines, and it seemed as though the blow were an aphrodisiac to the group festivities, but Brandon and I had three quart-size mason jars full of name-brand weed in front of us. After a few tokes any disappointments with the direction the night was taking were easily forgotten, and besides, I would join them when they were ready.

My brother and I remained upstairs alone for quite awhile, occasionally punctuating the silence between us with half-baked musings on the dilemma of freewill in a universe subject to physical laws, or the dilemma of "Freebird" versus

"Stairway to Heaven." My brother's background in philosophy and physics isn't as strong as mine, but he's as well versed as I am in music, and when I spotted an acoustic guitar in the corner I immediately took it up and began to play the opening few verses of each song so that a detailed analysis might be made. As I was pointing out to Brandon that each tune could be said to adhere to Poe's "Philosophy of Composition" in that the music and lyrics of both are subordinate to creating a unifying effect, Karen emerged at the top of the steps. She had changed into a long, flowing nightgown that had a neckline that plunged in a thin V-shape to her navel, the bottom half of gown slit on both sides up to her thighs.

Marijuana-- particularly the kind that has a pedigree-- doesn't exactly make one a quick wit. While it is easy to slip into lengthy and painfully detailed digressions about music, the cosmos, or ice cream, sudden changes in one's setting tend to be addressed with a degree of slowness and stupidity. Sadly, it was my brother who spoke first and said, "Damn."

I quickly snapped to attention (more than just mentally), lest Brandon's obviousness derail the night in some unforeseen fashion. "Are we having a slumber party?" I smiled, forgetting about my tooth.

"I heard you playing the guitar." Karen crossed the room, her nightgown trailing after her as thin veil of mist, and sat beside me. Her bare thigh brushed against me. "I really like the way you play."

"Thanks." I could achieve no greater response than that, as the blood had suddenly drained from my brain and was in rapid transit to lower circulatory regions.

"Why don't you come down and play with us now." She purred those words in such a tantalizing way that she could have been inviting me to my death and I would have gone

along just as willingly. But it was not my death I was going
to: I was being ushered into a basement where I would have
sex with two models (well, one was a former model, but
still...) and it was totally okay. I could not be punished for it,
and better yet I didn't have to buy an engagement ring. I was
also stoned senseless on the most premium weed I'd ever
smoked. Life was grand. I followed Karen to the top of the
steps where she turned and looked at my brother and said,
"Why don't you come, too? We've never had brothers here."

I was a little taken aback by this, but more so by my
brother's reaction: given the chance to have sex with a model
in the same room as me, I was sure he'd bail out just like I
would. *Thanks but no thanks.* Instead he practically leaped
over the plush sofa and began to follow us downstairs,
grinning wildly and not saying a word.

In the basement everyone was seated in a rough
approximation of a circle, chattering loudly and laughing. A
large sheet of plastic lay on the floor. The cocaine and the
coffee table were gone, and as we entered the room Harry
said, "Hey, I thought--" but Karen cut him short saying,
"We've never had brothers." Harry just shrugged his
shoulders and seemed to quickly forget about it, saying only:

"Well, Greg, let's show them how it's done." Harry stood
and took off his shirt and looked at my brother and me,
"Gentleman first, boys. That's how we do it for the ladies
here." If it got the girls hot I didn't mind stripping down for
their pleasure; my brother was hesitant, and sat immobile
while I stood and disrobed. I admit it was awkward having
him there, and it didn't help my penis presentation one bit.
His presence kept my dick limp and tiny, and when I looked
at him he just shook his head and chuckled. Harry and Greg
were greasing themselves with baby oil. With the exception
of their heads, their bodies were hairless, and they had the

toned look of men who spend time unreasonable amounts of time at a gym. Harry said, "Come on Brandon, no stragglers. Kevin, grease it up. You'll be next."

I picked up the baby oil and stared at it, perplexed, then looked at the rug of hair on my chest-- it was going to be an ugly mess momentarily. And then I said, "Next for what?"

"This!" Greg shouted, and flung his naked body into Harry's, whereupon they collapsed into a pile on the plastic, their cocks stiffening as they each tried to wrestle the other into submission. My brother stood up and left the basement quickly.

The women watched attentively, completely disinterested in my thin, ungreased frame, but enthralled by the scene taking place before them: two hunky men slipping over each other, occasionally grabbing the other's cock and yanking on it in as they maneuvered through some bizarre, homo-erotic, hand job wrestling match. To say that I was mortified would be an extreme understatement. I felt as though I were going to have a panic attack, and it was not the first time that the collapse of my fantasies had left me with such a feeling.

In the interest of full-disclosure, I must confess to another brush with group sex that happened so early in my erotic life that I was infinitely more unprepared for it than I was when I descended the stairs into Harry's basement and was caught up in that scene. The circumstances were actually not so different: a lot of alcohol, a fair amount of drugs, and horny people circulating in close proximity to one another. The big difference was that in the first instance, we were all in high school.

Someone's parents were out of town; it was mid-Spring, and those two factors combined with the impending close of the school year were enough to warrant a party. Actually, any of those things alone were enough to justify a Dionysian celebration, but such a triple-threat brought on even greater accomplishments in teenage debauchery. Kegs were obtained, liquor cabinets raided, parents' drug stashes pilfered-- no expense was spared in orchestrating one of those parties which is destined to take its place in the annals of local legend and reminisced about well beyond one's qualification for senior citizen discounts.

As is the case at such parties, all the boys were looking to get laid, and all the girls were equally interested in such activities but due to social customs were bound to be irritatingly coy about the business. Throughout the night gender specific huddles formed and reformed as territories were claimed, plans hatched and revised, and the complicated formalities of adolescent mating rituals undertaken. (Or it seemed complicated then; now I know the formula was: act like you don't want it and you'll get it. It was that simple, but the perpetually dancing hormones made it impossible for me to reason clearly.)

Invariably, there was always some girl (usually the least attractive of the bunch) who acted as the moral barometer of her immediate clique, weighing in on the various romantic treaties circulating, and usually stalling them in committee out of her own displeasure with being overlooked by the male faction. As the tactics of these girls were more often effective than not (the female brain being more developed in the area of higher reasoning than its male counterpart at this time in life), the politics of circumventing the gyno-guardian involved one of two approaches: someone putting the movies on the gatekeeper herself for the good of the team, or separating a potential partner from her pack. The latter of these two strategies was the preferred method, but neither of these plans were as well coordinated as I make out: only

through the lens of memory does the picture take on a
coherent shape, transforming the past riddles of courtship
into a banal replay of nearly everyone's shared adolescent
experience. We acted from instinct, our brains being
saturated with primordial hormones.

I usually fell into the role of the one who would act as a
decoy for the good of "the team." In truth there was no team.
Any of my immediate friends would have gladly blinded
every other guy there with a fire poker if he thought it would
get him laid. I would have done the same, but I was always
fairly sure that I wasn't getting laid; I wasn't the most
popular fellow in high school, and at this stage in my life I'd
only had one miserable, floundering experience with a
woman. It had been so terrible that I didn't even fantasize
about it when I jerked off. Plus I had a better vocabulary
than most of the other guys my age, and such a skill meant I
was a good conversationalist, and thus a better distraction.

But things went differently at this party. I was more in a
drinking mood, and reluctant to chat up the sober girl who
was mothering the prospective females. The host of the party
was into classic rock and not the hits of the day (quite a
relief, considering this was the late 80s, when music in
general just flat out *sucked*), and so I hovered near the keg,
bobbing my head to AC/DC and Nazareth.

By the talk that circulated as beers were being refilled, I
could tell that something of significance was afoot. The girl
every guy wanted, a new girl at school named Camille, was
being extremely flirty with all the boys-- those with and
without girlfriends. It was causing quite a stir, and whenever
a herd of young men gathered around the keg, the
conversation was drifted into a detailing of the various
positions and techniques each potential suitor might employ
if given the chance. The subject of the girls' talk was

understandably different: they were ready to kill the bitch.

My main reason in sticking to the keg and not circulating amongst the other guests was that I wanted my fair share of beer. Remember: we were all underage and so we couldn't just run out and get more when the keg dried up. Too many times I'd chipped in on the cost of a keg only to come away with fewer than three cups. I wasn't about to let that happen on this occasion, and while I held my ground firmly for a greater stretch of time than what was probably advisable, I eventually realized my bladder was about to rupture. I topped off my plastic cup of beer for the trip and began searching for a bathroom.

The house was large, and every door seemed to be locked; if it wasn't locked it opened onto a scene of couples making out or engaged in private conversation-- I was greeted several times with hostile stares and a string of profanities. I finally stumbled into a dark bedroom where a beacon of light shone from an open door in a corner that led to a bathroom. I entered, shut the door, and took a substantial piss-- a release of the bladder so necessary and pleasant that I let out a little moan of relief. As I was shaking off the last few drops, I heard voices in the bedroom outside. I didn't feel like being trapped in a bathroom while a couple fondled each other for hours on the other side of the door, so I made for a quick exit. As I entered the bedroom a guy's voice said:

"What the fuck? Keck! Dude! You are just in time."

Coming from the brightly lit bathroom into the dark bedroom, I had no idea what I was just in time for. The bathroom light illuminated four figures standing in a half circle, and after a few seconds I was able to make out that it was Jason, Brad, T.C., and John-- guys whom I hung out with from time to time, but none of them were what I would consider close friends.

"I said you four was okay, but I didn't say nothing about him."

I looked to my right, and half dressed on the bed lay Camille.

"Oh, come on," Jason said. "Keck's cool. What's one more?"

I started to say something, but my heart had begun racing, and the room seemed wobbly.

"Well, whatever. But I told you it had to be one at a time."

If Camille was angling for popularity amongst the boys at her new school, she was on a path destined for stardom. But something in her voice had a tone more of resignation than eagerness. Her presence on the bed seemed obligatory, as though she were a contract player in some adolescent studio of sexual imagination.

"Good deal, but Keck--" Jason turned his head toward me in the faint light and spoke as he undid his pants "-- you gotta go last."

"Okay," I said, and I leaned against the wall, completely disoriented by what was taking place. I, too, had dreamed of Camille since she first appeared in school, and I had often dreamed of group sex with Camille, but in my more typical fantasy that involved me as the lone male amongst a bevy of beauties. But opportunity arrived unannounced, and so I braced myself to take advantage of it anyway I could.

There was very little sexiness about the whole ordeal, though in retrospect it has taken on elements of appeal in my imagination that I know for a fact weren't there at the time; Camille's open legs were not an invitation of willing acceptance that welcomed each boy a little closer to manhood-- her panting cries of "fuck me" were not urgings to do just that, but rather a mantra to speed each guy toward a rapid finish. I had the notion at the time, though I am more certain of it now, that Camille's decision to be the center of a gang-bang was a direct result of her own desire to belong and be accepted. And that's a pretty simplistic rendering of the whole matter, but the truth often is that simple: people want to belong and be important and be loved, and sometimes we go about getting what we want in weird ways.

I wanted all those things, too, *and* Camille, but stressful situations are havoc on my digestive system, especially when I've been drinking. When the last of the four guys had finished and it was my turn-- alas, less than 10 minutes had elapsed since I'd left the bathroom; I'd been watching the digital clock next to the bed to see how long it took each guy as a way to measure my own manhood-- I felt myself on the edge of puking, and I could not produce an erection. Camille looked relieved, but that did not deter her from joining in the group mockery of my inability to step up to the plate and have sex in front of a bunch of other guys, like a real man.

"What are you, some kind of faggot?" she yelled as I lurched into the bathroom and unloaded the contents of my stomach into the toilet. I shut and locked the door and fell asleep on the cool linoleum floor, slipping out to my car before daylight, past the sleeping bodies strewn about the house. I worried the rest of the weekend that my limp performance would make the gossip rounds at school, but I overestimated my own importance in the wake of Camille's feat: thrilled by tales of an orgy, the grapevine was indifferent to my inept presence during the act.

Perhaps my failure to stiffen up some fourteen years before was at the root of my desire to know the slippery blending and taking of willing bodies, but I wasn't especially excited about doing battle with my demons in this manner. I looked at Lorraine, who smiled demurely at me, and then I gazed at the tangle of Harry and Greg on the floor in front of me. Without looking at me Harry reached up and put his hand on my thigh; I felt my penis trying to shrink into my abdomen. Harry's hand was stroking Greg's cock as they wrestled, and they paused in their struggle simultaneously as Harry addressed me, his hand never ceasing it's up and down motion:

"Hey man, what's wrong? You think this is some sort of gay thing? The girls just like a good show, man. It's not a gay thing-- our wives are right here watching. We just like to wrestle and fondle each other because it gets them hot. There's nothing gay about this, and when they get hot we fuck them and we watch each other-- it's all good."

I was confused, but not by his reasoning: I believed what he said about this whole scene not being gay; sexuality is far too complicated to be defined by whether or not you love to stroke someone else's cock, and however poorly phrased his argument may have been, he was essentially right.

Be that as it may, none of this changed my own stance on the cock stroking issue: I like mine, and I don't like my own cock being stroked by anyone who has one. The thought neither repulses nor arouses me; it is the same indifference I have when I think of the "Style" section of the newspaper: who cares?

I was willing to sit through this portion of the festivities, feigning interest (but not participating), as long as I was fucking the hot wives shortly thereafter. I clarified this point to make sure there wasn't a requirement of involvement in the first act of the floorshow:

"You mean you fuck each other's wives while you watch, but you don't have to--"

I didn't have a chance to finish my question before Harry stopped jerking on Greg's cock and looked at me grimly. "No, man. That's kind of fucked up. I got more respect for my wife than to let some other dude fuck her." He looked at Greg.

"No offense."

"None taken. I feel you."

In the midst of this discussion I'd missed Lorraine's exit from the room; the wives were holding hands on the couch and sipping their drinks, bright-eyed with their husbands' declaration of spousal devotion. These were some coke snorting, Greek-wrestling, nut cases, and they also had drawn a line in the sand: it just happened to be a little further out than mine. I stood slowly and said, "Would you all excuse me for a moment?" I headed back up the stairs, scooping my clothing from the floor as I did so. Before I reached the top of the staircase I heard Harry's merciless pumping of Steve's member begin again as Harry said, "What a fucking dick." I wasn't confused at all by his meaning.

My brother was staring at the television not like a person who is actually watching TV, but like a person who is looking at the television in order to avoid seeing his brother naked. As I dressed I said:

"Where's Lorraine."

"Outside smoking." His answer was robotic.

"Get your shit together; we're about to leave."

"Man," he said. "I've *had* my shit together."

Outside, Lorraine was smoking with hurried puffs, trying to repress a small, smug smile. She and I stood in the aura of the porch light while my brother walked to the car.

"What the fuck was that, Lorraine?" I was more genuinely puzzled than pissed; marijuana has a way of doing that.

She inhaled deeply and then exhaled as she turned to me and said coolly, "I said to buy me a ring, fucker, and I'd do anything you wanted, and what did you do? You gave me a fifty dollar gift card to Target." She puffed her cigarette again. "Besides, I thought you'd like that shit."

I stared toward the sky but the streetlights obscured the tapestry of stars that I knew to be shimmering overhead. "Target has some nice stuff," I said, and I walked to the car, Lorraine not far behind me behind me.

Eventually Lorraine's urgent desire to be married would manifest into an unceasing passive/aggressive rage, the culmination of which was her revelation about sleeping with my neighbor, Brian. But it would be several months before that would happen. In the meantime, I accepted her anger, because she was hot and knew how to make me come. It all seemed completely worthwhile when I was in the thick of it.

But on that morning, my brother and I left Lorraine at my apartment and took off in his car on the pretense of getting some breakfast. We drove downtown and through the city; the barricades marking the party from hours before had been set aside, the streets mostly swept clean-- small bits of trash and confetti still clung to the sidewalks as a light dusting of snow. Aside from the few people who still were obligated to be at work the roads were empty except for the two of us. We drove past the bank buildings that towered toward heaven, the gleaming new apartments like mushrooms sprouting up around them, the churches that hunkered humbly in the city's steel canyons, and we kept driving until the wide boulevards of asphalt dwindled into a trickle of ragged road that wound us to a fist of rock rising from the earth.

We left our car outside the gate to the park and took the shortest trail to the summit of Crowder's Mountain; the sky was violet, and a thin ribbon of white buffered the edge of the horizon, broken only by my city standing erect and mute in the distance.

I looked for the brightest star in the sky, but was met with

a band of shimmering satellites, and so instead of thinking of
the dead stars and their light that continues to travel long
after their collapse, I thought of the astronauts circling the
earth at that precise moment in the Russian space station.
Does the mania of fireworks sparkle beyond the
stratosphere? And who do the astronauts kiss at midnight,
and who cares anyway? I suspect that hovering above the
earth, one ceases to be concerned about earthly things; the
body begins to lose muscle mass when it's in space, which is
a beautiful concept: detached from the soil that holds us
firm, we begin to disintegrate, to fade into the universe. I
imagine the mind losing its sense of self, the disparity of
fantasy and reality finally merging, until dreams sweep up
the missing molecules of the body and the cosmos ripples as
the surface of a still lake broken by the return of a stone.

Uncollected Essays*

* Technically these essays should be called, "Things I Couldn't Figure Out How to Wedge into My Previous Books." However, while the essay about hand jobs was cut from *Oedipus Wrecked* because it stood out as stylistically different (and it was written with a more magazine sensibility in mind), the piece "Sleeping with Students" was nixed from *OW* because the publisher didn't wish to risk wading into any murky legal waters. It almost made its way into *AYTG?IM.K.*, but I cut it because it seemed tonally out of sync with the rest of the book. Besides, I thought it might make a book of its own someday. And someday, when the time is right, it probably will.

The Death of the Hand Job

In all the time I've spent engaging in sexual activity with other people, I have achieved orgasm via the blowjob route only once. Some men (and women) see this as my tragic flaw: a man obsessed with his penis, and yet unable to benefit from one of the great joys of having one. And while I have been grateful to every woman who has declared with soulful conviction that she will be the one to fellate me with such professionalism that my head will pop off, it's just really not my cup of tea. After thirty minutes of pointless head-bobbing, many women have raised up from my cock with a look of total failure (more like annoyance, actually). That is when I take their hand and explain to them the art that so many women have forgotten or lack completely: how to punch the bishop.

The first time I demonstrated this technique to a girl was in college. She seemed totally offended by my inability to come from the ministering of her mouth. When I clued her in on strange concepts such as "friction" and "velocity," she barked, "Why would you want me to jerk you off? Can't you do that yourself?" (It seems appropriate to point out that some men can actually blow themselves, and yet this apparently doesn't abate their desire to have others do it. My own failure at this activity came after I witnessed it in a porn film someone had leant me: a guy was getting head from a girl, then at the point of orgasm he rolled onto his back and sucked himself off. This seemed like a novel idea, but lacking patience in my youth, I gave the maneuver it's test run while working with "live rounds"—I wrenched out my back and developed a keen respect for keeping one's seed out of a girl's eyes.)

But it has been my experience that the college lass who protested against "manual operation" does not bear the burden of that sentiment alone. However, this takes up the position that all hands feel the same. Any guy who approached the challenge of ambidextrous whacking in his salad days could expound on the mystery of difference between his left and right hand, but when that hand belongs to someone else... it's almost as if you are discovering jerking off for the first time all over again.

Which is why my friend Andrea, who shares the self-bestowed title "Best Head" with many other contenders worldwide, won't give a hand job. "That's ridiculous," she told me. "What am I? Some little dink in junior high who's never seen a dick before? I'm not afraid to stare it in the face. I'm twenty-five for God's sake." Andrea, who is actually thirty-two, seems to have gotten part of it right. It *does* seem sort of juvenile to simply shake hands with the old hog— something you would do under a blanket when you were fifteen and your parents might walk in at any instant.

By that logic, though, it becomes puzzling why more women haven't mastered this technique. With all the people that claim to enjoy sexual encounters in public places, surely not everyone is having intercourse or going down on someone? I mean, it just seems like *someone* would have to have developed a utilitarian appreciation for the stealth and simplicity of a hand job. (Of course, there is one truly great hurdle of the hand job: if you're not used to that activity, it can old quite quickly. When I take the time to consider the amount of my life I have spent laboring over my dick, doing that stupid, international motion that everyone understands, it is a wonder that I don't have the forearms of a gorilla. Or at least one forearm of a gorilla.)

Considering this, I remembered what my friend Joel told me in college after he had begun having sex with men in addition to women: "Keck, you *think* a woman knows what she's doing, and some do, but get a bunch of boys together and naked and watch out." Based on this, I called up another friend of mine, who is gay, to see if the gender most familiar with the genitals in question might have some insight.

"Skip," I began matter-of-factly, "do you think gay men give more hand jobs than straight women?"

In the lengthy pause that followed I began to worry that Skip had hung up on me, but he eventually said, "I guess." Thus, riddle solved: it is a straight-woman thing.

Which is an absurd generalization. I've had several relationships with women who seemed to like giving a hand job. Carol, whom I dated my last year in graduate school, would lie on her back and use a two-handed grip as I straddled her. She confessed that she liked to "see it shoot." The same was true for Cathy when we dated as undergrads, but besides the visual appeal Cathy said she liked doing it because it made her feel more in control. (Although she could take this too far. In one aborted role-playing incident she said, "I'll be the vet—pretend to be a sheep I have to collect sperm from." I have had a distaste for wool ever since.) And Leslie preferred to do it because she claimed that giving head made her feel like a slut.

I feel this is an important distinction that ties to what Andrea said about feeling juvenile while giving a hand job: there is a level of sexual maturity that exists with oral sex that does not exist with manual stimulation. Hand jobs were probably far more common when adolescents were not targeted by marketers more concerned with profit than preserving innocence and decorum (I'm making huge leaps of logic here, so bear with me...). And not to suggest that there is anything indecorous about a lady deep-throating a gentleman, but it is certainly an activity more well suited for the experienced participant than the rookie. I'm sure most parents would be far more comfortable stumbling upon their kids experimenting with hands as opposed to mouths. But tales of oral sex amongst those as young as twelve and thirteen are not uncommon on the newsstands and daytime television. Headlines scream that is an epidemic, while researchers dig for answers that are ever elusive (although "teenagers are goddamned horny freaks" seems to be a tidbit of info often overlooked). The simple fact of hormones plus the internet is probably at the root of it all, if you want the simple truth.

And in this flood of information that permeates our culture about the ecstasy that awaits us in the chamber of "adult sexuality," the simple pleasures are forgotten. The death knell of the hand job as common sexual play is perhaps signaled for us all as soon as we cross the threshold into a mouth, or vagina, or ass. Or some sort of large gourd.

When was the last time you and your partner kissed for hours, but without the follow-up of intercourse? Where did those teenage-tongues go? Don't you remember that pleasure of little muscles in moist mouths straining against one another? And then, after days or weeks of fooling around, a hand strays below the waist, a zipper is drawn open, a bottle of lotion is fetched (although take it from a man with sensitive skin: be careful what you put on your penis, or any other area for that matter), and before you know it, you are about to soil your mother's parlor sofa. And then your partner says, "You know, my arm is getting tired…"

Sleeping with Students

It's 5:45 a.m. on Sunday, and I am lying in my bed, bald and scrawny and pale. I'm wearing boxers that hang loosely on me, and a t-shirt which says "Chicks dig scrawny pale guys." I am blinded by the cruelest light, the covers are ripped from me, and my girlfriend stands at the foot of the bed glaring at me. She is standing next to my ex-girlfriend, who is dressed like a slutty Catholic school girl, wearing a halter top, pleated skirt, fishnet stockings, and the most sadistic high heels I have possibly ever seen.

My girlfriend says flatly, "You fucked up." I am not sure what is going on, but I am grateful that neither of them are my students this semester.

I readjust my pillow and sit up in the bed, crossing my arms and legs and assuming a casual pose. My girlfriend, Jenny, does not let her menacing gaze drift from me. My ex-girlfriend, Belinda, lies down on the bed beside me looking hurt and alarmingly dangerous. I feel myself getting an erection, but it's obvious that the three-way I have dreamed about since my sexually angstful adolescence will not happen this morning. I move my hands to shield my arousal from my girlfriend, who is probably well aware that her jeans and sweater ensemble have not elicited this response from my dick.

"What's up?" I ask, but I am beginning to realize what is up, and I am not the least bit surprised by any of it.

When I first began teaching, as a graduate student at a quasi-Ivy League, upstate New York university, I made a vow to myself that I would never cross the line separating the student/teacher relationship. I made this vow shortly after a terrifying seminar on sexual harassment sponsored by the university (which promised a fate for violators that fell just short of a brief internment in some upstate New York version of a death camp), and just before I met my first class: it was packed solid with women brazenly bearing their flesh in the lingering heat of late summer. Because I was fresh in town, I knew no one, and so I spent my first weeks there on my knees on the hardwood floor of my apartment, like some masochistic monk, taking out temptation on my cock. I imagined one tutoring session after another that collapsed into a pornographic pile of teacher and student entwined in my own private version of what the University referred to ambiguously as the "spiral curriculum." And one student in particular—Donna Berkowitz, a wonderful cliché of a Jewish girl from New Jersey—evoked such a deep desire in me with her ample bosom and well-sculpted nose lending her voice an erotic whine, I had to sit down whenever she spoke in class because of the monstrous hard-on she gave me. (She earned a less than favorable grade in my class, which I cavalierly altered two years later under the pretense that I might be able to seduce her with my generosity—this was not the case.)

Yet as much as the co-eds sent me home every evening in a most aggravated state, I never drifted across that boundary of unceasing desire. It was not until my third year as a graduate teaching assistant that opportunity presented itself in such a way that I was bound to seize it whether I was conscious of the prospect or not.

A requirement in my classes was that my students keep a journal. It is with some amount of shame that I admit I was wholly aware at the time that my exclusive interest in their journals was to possibly learn those lascivious details of their lustful undergraduate years. My own college career was a deep disappointment (I started out to become a priest of all things, and contrary to the myth, few women I encountered were willing to risk the possibility of eternal damnation in order to live out their fantasy luring a man-of-the-cloth-in-training to temptation). Thus, I hoped that by having my students write about their own lives I would be able to reinvent my own, at least in my sexual imagination.

On my first read-through of the Spring semester journals, Cindy Lowell, a delicate, nineteen-year-old red head who seemed to have a perpetual runny nose and a tongue ring that caused her to lisp slightly, had written a note to me that she felt we'd get along quite well socially. However, she concluded that such an outing might be problematic as she wasn't sure of the rules that governed such relationships. Since it was common knowledge that two of the philosophy professors were living with students with whom they were romantically involved, I didn't think it would be such a disaster if Cindy sported her fake I.D. one night and joined me at a cigar bar downtown.

After only one beer, Cindy and I retreated to my apartment where, as she reclined on the pool table I had purchased from Cher's former road manager, she wriggled out of her hip-hugging jeans and revealed to me the first bald pussy I'd ever glimpsed in person. It was as magnificent as I had imagined it would be, and I felt as though I were finally standing face-to-face with the Mona Lisa's curious smile after a lifetime of puzzling over it in books.

Cindy's body was alabaster, and her nipples perked up as my fingers found their way softly around her small frame. It was the one and only time I ever had sex on the pool table (for some reason my fear of ruining the tournament quality carpet was temporarily assuaged that night), and it stands as

one of the defining moments in my life. Up until that point I
had lacked completely the ability to ejaculate with a woman
during our initial intercourse, unless I took matters into my
own hands, which never made any girl feel as though she was
as sexy and as beautiful as I claimed. It was (sadly) the first
encounter I had with a woman where I truly felt like a man.

When I came, I pulled out and sent great streams of
semen all across her. Whatever virility I experienced during
the event notwithstanding, as soon I shook the last quiver of
release from me, I flipped out. I couldn't comprehend what I
had just done. I had standards, didn't I? And wasn't this a
flagrant violation of them? I was overcome with a
strangeness similar to the first time I experienced an orgasm
in front of a woman. I was awash with guilt and anxiety—and
one can only begin to imagine what unspeakable horror in
my infancy involving (more than likely) a rectal thermometer
might have lead to this reaction. As a drop of semen made a
slow, clinging descent from the tip of my penis and down
towards Cindy's navel, I said:

"This was a bad idea."

Her face clouded over quickly, and she began to scream:

"OH MY GOD! YOU'RE NOT GOING TO ASK ME TO
LEAVE AFTER YOU JUST FUCKED ME ARE YOU? I FEEL
LIKE SUCH A FUCKING WHORE! FUCK YOU, YOU
FUCKING FUCK!"

I felt my penis go cold and limp in my hand, and I
thought about the come that was drying on Cindy's chest and
neck.

"Would you like me to make you some toast?"

She stared at me blankly. I tried again, this time with
something less nurturing:

"It's not you; it's me."

She seemed to understand this, and so I began to explain

the terrible misfortune that we had experienced together, how it would be bad for both of us if this became public, how it never should have happened, and that while I appreciated her interest in me, it would be best if this encounter were forgotten. When I was done she looked at me and sighed:

"You're nothing like I thought you would be. I'm really disappointed."

I refrained from telling her that she was not the first woman to come to this conclusion. We both dressed in silence, and when she was ready I walked her sheepishly to the door.

I tried to leave things on an up note. I reminded her that she had a paper due tomorrow, but under the circumstances I would consider giving her an extension if she needed it. She smiled. I thought about kissing her goodnight, then decided against it. I watched her walk across the street to her car, then I turned to go back inside. From behind me I heard:

"I MEAN REALLY DISAPPOINTED, KECK! YOU SUCK LIKE I'VE NEVER SEEN!"

I didn't turn around. Cindy never showed back up in class, and when I did see her on campus she pivoted as if on pointe, and promptly walked in the opposite direction. I gave her an "A" at the end of the semester, felt lucky to have escaped being caught, and decided that if I had at least learned something from the experience then it wasn't a total waste.

I now conclude that the experience was a total waste. Should I have expected anything less? In the simple world of pop-psychologists, I was only behaving exactly as I was supposed to. I was chasing the archetype of romance, the model by which I was to set all standards. My entire upbringing is filled with fairy tales of romance between my mother and father, a romance that began when she was a

student in 1968 in his history class at a small, religiously
affiliated college nestled in the mountains of North Carolina.
   It would have been a great help had I recognized this
obvious comparison prior to taking a job as an adjunct
professor at a small, religiously affiliated college that was
also sunk into the backwoods of the Old North State. Even
had the fact crossed my mind at the time, however, I would
have dismissed it: I was dedicated to becoming a full-time
faculty member, and I was going about my business, by the
book.
   My return to the South was nothing short of a culture
shock. Upon acceptance of my position at the college, I was
asked to sign a form stating that I was a practicing Christian.
I had no reservations about this: if you're paying me, I'll sign
a form saying I was the sole mastermind behind the
Holocaust. But for the record, it had been so long since I'd
set foot in a church that I avoided the prospect at all costs for
fear of being immediately incinerated once I crossed the
threshold.
   Besides making sure (by God) that their instructors were
of the sort of strong Christian influence that they wanted
around their students, it was campus policy that men and
women were not allowed to engage in displays of public
affection. Private affection was also off limits, but
understandably harder to enforce. Thus, males and females
were housed in different buildings, and visitation was limited
more or less to those hours of the day when the sun
illuminates all dark corners where sin could be hiding out.
Also, if a man and a woman were in a room alone, it was
mandated that the door to that room should be open. This
went for teachers, staff, and students. (Later I would learn
that this extended so far as to include visiting family
members, which shouldn't have surprised me in a state

where I had once been encouraged to ask my first cousin on a date.)

Despite the overall atmosphere that at any moment one could be visited by the Inquisition, I welcomed a chance at discipline and purity. I really wanted to have a bland, middle-class life, to immerse myself in a world that existed only in books. I was grateful to be on a campus where students openly discussed their total dedication to a life spent in service of the Lord. The girls were maddeningly delicious, but they were single-minded about their commitment to a sin-free, Christian life.

The second week of classes a rather bookish girl (and a very outspoken Star Wars aficionado), Elizabeth, appeared in my office. After some idle chit-chat about class there was a long, uncomfortable lull in the conversation. I sensed Elizabeth had something on her mind, so I sat behind my desk with my eyebrows raised.

"Do you ever watch *Sex and the City*?" she finally asked.

I had to confess that I didn't watch it on any regular basis, but that I had seen a few episodes.

"Did you see the one about the politician who wants to pee on Sarah Jessica Parker?"

"Yes." I wasn't quite sure where this was leading, but I assumed that as a student at a Christian institution she was about to launch into a litany regarding the morality of such an act as based on her readings of the scriptures.

"What did you think about that?"

Honestly, I had thought nothing of it. It neither appealed to me, nor disgusted me, which is why when later that night Elizabeth showed up at my apartment dressed conservatively, and after a few sips of white zinfandel shed her clothing to lay down in my shower waiting for my warm stream of urine to flow over her, I attempted to comply.

Whatever hang-ups she had about patriarchal figures and her self-worth had been decided long before I came along, and so I didn't feel especially heinous as I tickled the tip of my penis in an attempt to coax a good, long piss from it. I had been drinking water for the previous several hours, and I could feel the ache for release in my kidneys and bladder.

Nothing was happening though. Elizabeth kept alternating her anxious gaze from my flaccid member to my face. She would occasionally utter the encouraging phrase ("Come on, piss on me, I'm you're little whore," etc.), but for the most part remained silent. I admit I was nervous. I also admit that I have had problems my entire life when it comes to urinating under pressure. I can't begin to recount the number of times I have been at some concert, waiting in a line for the bathroom that flowed at the pace of Silly Putty, worrying that I might wet myself, only to discover as I finally stood in front of the urinal that the pressure to pee quickly and move on was just too much. I would freeze-up. I would try to pretend I was alone, in my own bathroom, with the nurturing hum of the exhaust fan overhead and a soothing, diffused light. But it was always to no avail, and so I would fake the shake-off, flush the toilet, and walk away completely disgusted with myself.

Eventually I turned the shower on, hoping that the warm water might relax me. To Elizabeth's credit she kept up a good face, never criticizing, but always provoking me to let her have it, because she had been bad and deserved to be treated like a filthy slut. In my mind, though, I kept thinking how silly this all was, how it held no allure for me, and how I just felt rather sorry for an attractive, young girl who sought out some sort of connection with another human being via *this* avenue. Finally, Elizabeth, in a cause and effect miscalculation, began to masturbate. I suddenly sprouted an erection, and peeing was out of the question. Before I could offer to help her finish, the water went cold.

When we were out of the shower I suggested that next time we try something more traditional. She said:

"Oh, I don't have sex. That's a sin. At least until I'm married."

And then she dressed and left to meet her fiancé at church. Eventually that same fiancé would break into my apartment one night, lying in wait for my return so he could kick the shit out of me. Fortunately, I am a heavy pot smoker, and I often fall asleep in strange places and never make it to my own bed. Such was the case the night that the frustrated fiancé intruded upon my domicile, but he eventually was able to have me fired for being a pornographer because of the subject nature of most of my writing. For the longest time I sympathized with his anger: I doubt I would want a strange man making an attempt, however feeble and willingly received, to urinate on my fiancé. Months after my dismissal, I discovered he had no knowledge of the aborted golden shower; he was incensed over the white zinfandel his fiancé and I had shared. Southern Baptists are funny that way.

I was able to pick up adjunct work fairly quickly at the local community college. It speaks volumes about my knowledge of my subject area, or the sad state of American education, that I was hired on the spot while completely stoned. I had ripped about twenty bong hits prior to the interview—perhaps the best interview I've ever had—and chatted away merrily about my love of teaching disinterested youths the merits of the five paragraph essay.

After having been fired for being a pornographer, and enduring the humiliation of being "pee shy," I felt that I had more or less hit rock bottom. To make matters worse, I wasn't even able to afford the quality of cannabis that I had grown accustomed to. It comes as no surprise then that I did not take my position as an adjunct instructor at a community college very seriously, which is why when one of my students called me up after the first class meeting to ask if she could come to my apartment for some tutoring I was more than willing to work overtime for free.

Fiona was a petite, dirty blond who dressed like a hippy, and I have always had a weakness for hippy girls: nothing about them seems overly processed or fortified with preservatives. And despite everything that had happened to me up until that point, I in no way saw myself as a man with whom women were eager to have sex. I spent the hours before her arrival drinking Coors and smoking one joint after another, until I was seriously on the brink of being more aware of the earth spinning than I ever care to be. When Fiona arrived at my apartment she seemed embarrassed; I was doing my best to seem as cool as possible, but it's hard to seem very cool when remaining upright is problematic.

I made matters entirely worse by not getting right down to it. A professor more experienced than I (and perhaps tenured as well) might have thrown the young, nubile body of Fiona against the wall immediately and plunged into her. I wanted to at least collect enough of the community college's meager paychecks in order to pay rent for a few months, so I made sure that things were as Kosher as possible first. I offered her a drink, asked her about her family, and what she was studying. She sat on the floor in front of me, shifting positions every now and again, and seemingly making a point of not disguising the fact that she had no underwear on under her skirt. The tension of the situation kept my stomach in knots.

Finally I said, "I see you're not wearing any underwear."

Fiona looked up at me, surprised, then opened her legs and hiked her skirt up. She spread her labia and said: "I have a pretty pussy, don't I?"

The night overwhelmed me at that moment, and I puked all over her pretty pussy. I do not have a high tolerance for alcohol, or sexual tension, and the combination of the two usually unmasks me as the neurotic mess I truly am. Fiona showered and left that night in some sweatpants and a t-shirt of mine, and I cuddled up in bed with a bottle of Pepto. But she didn't lose interest. That should have been a warning signal of some sort.

Fiona made a nest of my apartment, which would have been fine if her love-child dress code accurately reflected her musical tastes. Instead, she blasted songs consisting of irritatingly out of tune guitars while walking around the house as though her womb were swelling, telling me that she couldn't wait to "become a mother." Her assertion that she was on the pill became a point of skepticism for me.

After a few weeks she took me to meet her father, a brutal stump of a man who couldn't have been much more than 5'1". Standing modestly over six feet, I towered above him and tried to be very aware of that fact so as not to come off as superior in any way. Immediately he said:

"Is my daughter getting an A in your class?"

Out of habit I fell into professional mode:

"Well, she's doing fine in the class so far, but she has a few issues with her writing which need to be worked out. I think if she puts her mind to it, she'll do fine on the final, and there's no reason why she couldn't make an A."

"She's been sleeping at your apartment. I imagine she'll get an A."

I decided right then that trouble was brewing.

I started staying at my office more, to avoid going back to

my apartment and being cornered by Fiona. She started lingering after class and coming to see me during my office hours. After a few close calls where she announced a bit too loudly that she would see me back at home, I went to the only place I could: the men's room. I closed myself in a stall and graded papers, caught up on my reading, and even fell asleep on occasion—though I tried not to. I harbored a secret fear that the graffiti on the stall wall advertising homosexual encounters in the visitors' locker room of the field house would somehow imprint on my forehead and not wash off. Finally, during a night of love-making when Fiona cooed for me to fill her with my "thick baby batter," I hopped up from the bed and announced, "Fiona, I want to pee on you."

I helped her pack her things, dropped her off at her father's house, and watched as she walked to the door where he was waiting for her. He glared at me, then took her into his arms and held her in a way that made me frightfully uncomfortable and once again glad to be out of such a sticky mess.

The following semester when I began teaching at The Art School I reasserted my personal conviction that despite my parents' thirty-year odyssey together, it was altogether impossible in this day and age for anything good to come from relations with the student body. Besides, if I had learned nothing else from my previous encounters, at the very least I should have grasped the fact that young women *do* find me attractive, and that statistically most of those young women did not attend the school at which I taught. My reasoning, however sound it may seem, would only have been slightly less accurate had I based it on the wisdom gleaned from petrified goose turds.

From the very beginning of my tenure at The Art School I was made to feel like a piece of raw meat dangled before starving jackals. Whereas my prior liaisons with studious nymphs had stunned me by their actual occurrence, I was constantly aware in my new position that whenever I said the word there were several eager young ladies willing to deliver. Nothing could have been more mind-boggling, save for growing a cactus on my forehead as I slept.

I do not mean to sound insincere in my claims of bewilderment at my students' lust. The simple fact of the matter is that anyone who knows me will substantiate the claim that, in the non-academic universe, I am a total butterfingers where courtship is concerned. Before becoming a bonafide college instructor, I dated intermittently, had relationships that never fully satisfied me (or my partners), and spent the majority of my time alone and depressed. Since then I have had the best sex of my life, with the most beautiful women I have ever dated, and they've all been my students. I am at once repulsed and fascinated by this realization.

Why is this? When I was a student I had a swashbuckler's main of thick, luscious hair, and now I endure my friends' unrelenting repertoire of premature baldness humor. While I've always been lean, years of getting stoned and entranced by the Discovery Channel have turned me into the worst of all creatures: the out-of-shape thin guy. As I've gotten older, my problems with depression have made me a rather difficult individual to be around. I owe more money than I'm comfortable thinking about. My penis, once a great source of aesthetic pride, has lost its looks a bit from too many allergic reactions to scented lotions. This being the case, it makes perfect sense why I am a bachelor in the world of bankers and bartenders.

But I am none of these things when I teach. When I am in front of a classroom, I am in charge. I am confident, I am charming, I know what I'm talking about. I make people laugh. I help people. I tell them they are doing a good job, that they are going to be okay, and if they aren't going to be okay, I let them know that I'll do what I can to help them fix it. And if they are attractive and of the female persuasion, then I am all the more likely to help them as much as I can.

During my year of teaching at The Art School I have managed to keep things under control—for the most part. The circumstances I currently find myself in—an early morning interrogation by my current and former sexual partner—lead me to believe that perhaps the amount of control I thought I wielded has diminished considerably. I watch as my girlfriend boxes up her possessions in the early hours of the morning, assisted by my ex-girlfriend. When I get up from the bed they stop what they are doing and observe me like an alligator whose eggs they are stealing. I walk past them and to the kitchen where I begin to make coffee.

My first semester at The Art School I walked around a corner only to hear Belinda, my ex-girlfriend, saying that whenever she heard me read in class she wanted to immediately fall to her knees and suck my cock. She made this statement the day after I had read a portion of Frederick Exley's *A Fan's Notes* to the class (and it was my sincere wish that Exley had gotten more than a few blow jobs out of that story in his day). I ignored this comment and went about my business. During a meeting with her towards the end of the semester, which was supposed to focus on her final research paper, Belinda detailed her dissatisfaction with the size of her current boyfriend's penis, using her cell phone to illustrate the length and girth that her beau lacked. I remained as professional as one could under the circumstances, and pointed out to her that she would certainly find someone who would fulfill her in more than just a physical way. As I said those words, though, I was taking mental notes as to the model of cell phone she had so that I could see (at a more convenient time) whether or not I measured up.

After she had exited my course for the semester, Belinda relentlessly pursued me. I shrugged her off. It wasn't out of arrogance that I kept this beauty at bay—had she possessed a greater sense of self-esteem Belinda could have easily made a living on the fashion runway—but rather the fact that I genuinely love—loved—my job, and at the time it seemed foolish to squander all of that over the temptation of forbidden fruit.

But it was becoming too much. Each day at school Belinda wore an outfit more revealing than the day before, and it was not long before I found myself jerking off as silently as possible in the bathroom stall next to the one where the Dean was taking a crap. It is a sad thing to have to ejaculate beside your boss as he lets loose a long, slow, staccato fart.

I was unwilling to yield to Belinda's seduction because I felt like a fuck-up due to my prior indiscretions, and now that I was making a full-time salary and had health insurance I wasn't about to break any rules. So I checked the rules to find a way around them, and there, on page thirty-four of the faculty handbook was the loophole I longed for: "... sexual relationships between faculty and students whom they teach or supervise are prohibited." I needed no clarification of that policy: *whom they teach or supervise*—Belinda was not in my class, never would be again, and I was never in a position to supervise her. Certainly I wouldn't be fucking her on my desk for all to see, but I surmised that, operating under the cloak of discretion, the policy gave me a green light to satiate my desires.

It was only a scant few hours after educating myself on the school's policy that I invited Belinda over and found myself tangled up, for what I hoped would be the last time, with one of my (former) students. I had never had a beautiful woman so willing to succumb to every whim that was born of my loins, and when she magically produced a vibrator and began rubbing it around my balls and ass as I fucked her over a mirror I thought I had found the woman of my dreams.

I am a finicky individual, however, and there is one quality a woman must possess in order to date me: the same unceasing desire to smoke pot and dance while listening to The Grateful Dead. (The utter absurdity of this characteristic is not lost on me.) Belinda possessed neither of these characteristics, and when I took her to a bluegrass festival where she elegantly and coolly smoked cigarettes and looked completely unamused the entire time, I knew it was time to call it quits.

Besides, as hot as the sex with Belinda was (and it truly was the stuff that dreams are made of), something just wasn't clicking with her. I began to notice that her sole desire was to fulfill every one of my desires, and that was an attitude that I didn't warm up to all that well. For starters, it reminded me of my mother. Also, my parents doted on me so much in my formative years that I have developed a rather unpleasant sense of entitlement—I try in my heart of hearts to be selfless and loving to all creatures, but if someone gives me the impression that they will wait on me hand and foot, well, by golly, who am I to turn down such an act of submission?

It makes me queasy to think that the ways in which we relate to one another as human beings are simply behaviors programmed into us when we all lacked the ability to reason whether what we were learning was right or not. In considering every relationship I have pursued with a student, what I see is people (including me) fumbling for some semblance of familiarity with their romantic quests. (Also, it helps to recall that every single student I've slept with at some point has unnervingly referred to me as "daddy," and usually while my cock was inside them or dangling above their heads.) I made an attempt to not exercise the programming I had received as a child: my parents are still locked in a relationship that is unequal; my father is still the Professor, my mother is still his willing student. It is this imbalance of power that occasionally erodes the structure of happiness they have erected. My father wants to be in charge, my mother still longs for the independence from her mentor that each student should always seek, and I have been a casual observer of this all my life. Fortunately, one doesn't need to see every option to know the one they've been witnessing isn't the best.

It was at that same bluegrass festival that I ran into Jenny, a girl who was in the same class as Belinda the previous semester. When Jenny offered me a joint as she began to kick up a little hoedown action of her own, I felt myself swoon. That loophole in the policy applied to her as well. The following day was Belinda's birthday, and I knew I could never break up with her then. So I ended things the day after her birthday, which may have been a terrible thing to do, but I figured it was better to break up with her than cheat on her.

That same logic, however, did not apply to Jenny. Jenny was nothing less than wonderful, but Belinda wouldn't let me go that easily, and being the miserable weak-willed sap that I am I allowed her to hang-on. And so I kept going back, back to her breasts, which were as magnificent and well proportioned as any breasts I have ever glimpsed. (For a time I considered photographing them and sending the photos to the National Association of Plastic Surgeons with a note indicating that any breast augmentation that yielded results different from the enclosed photo was a failure.) I kept going back because Belinda would call me on the phone, beg to be fucked like a little whore, would beg for my come on her face, would delight me with tales of her day-long masturbation sessions during which she thought only of my cock in her mouth. And despite the fact that I knew I was just some surrogate for that figure of power that she longed to have dominate her, I couldn't say no. I do not have the inner resources to deny such supplication. On the other hand, Jenny never said those kinds of things, but it didn't matter: I fell so completely in love with Jenny, because something in her stirred my soul. Also, that girl can take a bong hit.

Naturally, she found out. I do not make claims of being very smart or clever, let alone the master of discretion. Also, Belinda finally got pissed that I would only meet her in the afternoons; she felt she was entitled to a night on the town. But Jenny stayed with me, not that I deserved her. She told me that she could forgive me, but that meant never lying to her again. She said she wanted a relationship built on trust, and that meant treating her as an equal, and with respect. It would seem like the obvious course to take in any relationship; I'm surprised how difficult it is for everyone (especially me) to get that.

But I lied to her again anyway, and this is why I'm sitting at the kitchen table now at this unholy hour with an erection that is becoming increasingly painful. I lied about a phone call. Belinda called, I spoke with her briefly, and when Jenny asked me who it was I lied. I lied because I didn't want to argue about why Belinda had called, which was simply to say hello. (Also, *Buffy the Vampire Slayer* was about to come on television, and I can't have a serious discussion when that show is on.) So by some fluke they met at a party, which I failed to attend, having been slain earlier by a bong I refer to affectionately as "The Kevorkian." One thing lead to another, my lie about the phone call came out, and now all I can think about is how fucking hot my ex looks in that Catholic school girl outfit, and how just touching her would send a rocket of jism from my dick straight to the moon. But she is not the woman I love, and this presents a dilemma.

Jenny has packed her things and gone, leaving Belinda here. When Belinda has gone to the bathroom, I call Jenny's cell phone and leave a message telling her that I understand why she has packed her things, but that I love her. I tell her that I do not care about anything but her, that even though the faculty handbook leaves room for assuming this relationship is okay, I'm going to the Dean first thing the next day and telling him about the two of us because I want everyone to know how much I love her.

When Belinda returns from the bathroom she is completely naked. My cock pops through the flap in my boxers, and she says:

"Well, someone is certainly glad to see me."

Like so many other occasions, I am without an intelligible response.

"Look," she says, "I know we never had that much in common, but no one makes me come like you. So you can have what you want with her, do whatever, but don't stop fucking me. This can be just about sex, if that's what you want." She places her hands on my thighs, leans to my ear and says, "Isn't that what you want, daddy?"

Before I can answer, the phone rings out like an alarm.

* * *

I write these words sitting in my car in front of The Art School, which I was forced to resign from last week. Apparently there was another policy, in another handbook, which I was never given. There were no loopholes in that one. I was actually given notice in the middle of my last class on Monday that I should collect my personal belongings before I left. It was a good day to be lecturing on *A Tale of Two Cities*.

I am here now because Jenny totaled her car, and so I must drive her everyday to the place where I no longer work, and then drive there again to pick her up. I park at the edge of campus, where the girls pass by my car and do not take a second look at me. I do not look at them for very long either, but instead return my gaze quickly to the classified section of the paper, hoping there has been an opening for an instructor of English Literature at the all-male parochial school.

Acknowledgments

I try my level best to avoid pandering when it comes to thanking people where a book is concerned. After all, in most instances a book is a private matter—if other people have any worthwhile involvement during the writing process, it is probably because they gave the author refuge and comfort when he cracked up during the middle of the book, or when he fell to pieces thinking about starting the book, or when he finally finished the goddamned book and then went all to hell. While assembling this collection I was kept on the straight and narrow by Chad Snyder: It was rough weather for a while, but we do not speak of such brushes with peril, do we, old friend?

Hail Eris!

About the Author

Kevin Keck is the author of the books *Oedipus Wrecked* and *Are You There God? It's Me. Kevin.* His work has appeared in *The New York Quarterly, Details, Maxim,* and other fine literary magazines. You can find him on the internet at www.thekeck.com.